FRIENDLY ADVICE

COMPILED AND EDITED BY
JON WINOKUR

Dutton • New York

DUTTON
Published by the Penguin Group
Penguin Books USA Inc., 375 Hudson Street, New York,
New York 10014, U.S.A.
Penguin Books Ltd, 27 Wrights Lane, London W8 5TZ, England
Penguin Books Australia Ltd, Ringwood, Victoria, Australia
Penguin Books Canada Ltd, 2801 John Street,
Markham, Ontario, Canada L3R 1B4
Penguin Books (N.Z.) Ltd, 182-190 Wairau Road, Auckland 10, New Zealand

Penguin Books Ltd, Registered Offices: Harmondsworth, Middlesex, England

First published by Dutton, an imprint of Penguin Books USA Inc.

First Printing, September, 1990
10 9 8 7 6 5 4 3 2 1

Copyright © Jon Winokur, 1990
Illustrations copyright © Seymour Chwast, 1990
All rights reserved

 REGISTERED TRADEMARK—MARCA REGISTRADA

LIBRARY OF CONGRESS CATALOGING IN PUBLICATION DATA
Winokur, Jon.
    Friendly advice: wise, witty, and irreverent counsel / compiled and
edited by Jon Winokur.
        p.   cm.
    ISBN 0-525-24906-0
    1. Quotations, English.   2. Life skills—Quotations, maxims, etc.
3. Life skills—Humor.   4. American wit and humor.   I. Title.
PN6083.W56   1990
082-dc20   90-34421
                                                               CIP

Printed in the United States of America
Set in Bookman
Designed by Barbara Huntley

IN MEMORY OF ROSE BELMONT

CONTENTS

ACKNOWLEDGMENTS

Many thanks to Peter Bell, Karen and Reid Boates, Harlan Ellison, Norrie Epstein, Barbara Huntley, Margo Kaufman, Merle Kessler, John Leo, Constance Lofton, Gary Luke, Susan Nethery, Laurence and Irene Peter, Beth Siniawsky, Nancy Steele, Morris Taub, LuAnn Walther, Elinor Winokur, and Mark Wolgin. I'm grateful to the late Phyllis McGinley for the following friendly advice:

> *You'd better compile a collection*
> *Of words that another has wrote.*
> *It's the shears and the glue*
> *Which will compensate you*
> *And fashion a person of note.*
> *For poets have common companions,*
> *Their fame is a wraith in the mist.*
> *But the critics all quarrel*
> *To garland with laurel*
> *The brow of the anthologist, my son*
> *The brow of the anthologist!*

INTRODUCTION

This isn't a manual, a guide, or a how-to book. It's a collection of quotations and anecdotes filled with unusual and humorous advice—*friendly* guidance, authoritative but not authoritarian, consisting not of ponderous prescriptions but lighthearted suggestions. *Friendly* advice, but not necessarily *good* advice.

There's a difference. Good advice is condescending, humorless, and usually benefits only the giver. People tend to ignore it. Friendly advice, on the other hand, is sometimes frivolous, often ironic, and usually benefits the recipient. It is happily optional. It doesn't command or demean, it cajoles. It inveigles you with felicity of expression, arrests your natural resistance with humor or substance or poetry, and painlessly inoculates you with wisdom.

These quotations speak directly to the reader on a wide variety of subjects (Acting, Ageing, Baseball, Drink, Gambling, Love, Marriage, Politics, Sex, Success), often from unexpected sources (Groucho Marx, John Gotti, Albert Einstein, Malcolm Forbes, Andy Warhol, Ted Williams, Miss Piggy). Some, especially those in the "Best Advice I've Ever Received" and "Words to Live By" sections, were submitted especially for this book by various correspondents. The rest of the some, 1,300 quotations represent the amiable wisdom of the ages from artists, writers, scientists, clergymen, scholars, physicians, sports heroes, businessmen, actors, and statesmen.

So if you're in the market for cheerful insight—on your own terms—*Friendly Advice* may be just what you're looking for. And if at this very moment you're considering whether to buy this book, I'd advise you to do so immediately. If you like.

—J.W.
Pacific Palisades, California
November 1989

Advice, *n.* The smallest current coin.

AMBROSE BIERCE

It is always a silly thing to give advice, but to give good advice is absolutely fatal.

OSCAR WILDE

Good but rarely came from good advice.

LORD BYRON

The advice of their elders to young men is very apt to be as unreal as a list of the hundred best books. OLIVER WENDELL HOLMES

No one wants advice—only corroboration.

JOHN STEINBECK

We ask advice, but we mean approbation.

CHARLES CALEB COLTON

Advice is what we ask for when we already know the answer but wish we didn't. ERICA JONG

When we ask advice, we are usually looking for an accomplice. MARQUIS DE LAGRANGE

Advice is like snow; the softer it falls the longer it dwells upon, and the deeper it sinks into the mind. COLERIDGE

Advice is seldom welcome. Those who need it most, like it least. SAMUEL JOHNSON

In matters of religion and matrimony I never give advice; because I will have no man's torments in this world or the next laid to my charge. LORD CHESTERFIELD

Don't give a woman advice: one should never give a woman anything she can't wear in the evening. OSCAR WILDE

A good man giving bad advice is more dangerous than a nasty man giving bad advice. CONOR CRUISE O'BRIEN

Never trust the advice of a man in difficulties. AESOP

○-○

Madam, we took you in order to have children, not to get advice. CHARLES XI OF SWEDEN (to his wife in response to her pleas on behalf of one of his subjects)

○-○

Distrust interested advice. AESOP

We may give advice, but we cannot inspire conduct. LA ROCHEFOUCAULD

In giving advice seek to help, not to please, your friend. SOLON

Whatever your advice, make it brief. HORACE

A never-failing way to get rid of a fellow is to tell him something for his own good. KIN HUBBARD

The only thing to do with good advice is to pass it on. It is never of any use to oneself.
OSCAR WILDE

A good scare is worth more to a man than good advice. ED HOWE

About the worst advice you can give to some people is, "Be yourself." TOM MASSON

Nobody can give you wiser advice than yourself.
CICERO

How is it possible to expect that mankind will take advice, when they will not so much as take warning? JONATHAN SWIFT

Old people like to give good advice to console themselves for no longer being able to provide bad examples. LA ROCHEFOUCAULD

If someone gives you so-called good advice, do the opposite; you can be sure it will be the right thing nine out of ten times.
ANSELM FEUERBACH

When a man comes to me for advice, I find out the kind of advice he wants, and I give it to him.
JOSH BILLINGS

The worst waste of breath, next to playing a saxophone, is advising a son. KIN HUBBARD

The best way to give advice to your children is to find out what they want and then advise them to do it. HARRY S TRUMAN

○-○

The German poet Otto Erich Hartleben consulted a doctor who advised him to give up smoking and drinking. "That will cost you three marks," said the doctor. "I'm not paying," replied Hartleben, "because I'm not taking your advice."

○-○-○-○-○-○-○-○-○ ○-○

The art of giving advice is to make the recipient believe he thought of it himself. FRANK TYGER

What you do not use yourself, do not give to others. For example: advice. SRI CHINMOY

If a man knows where to get good advice, it is as though he could supply it himself. GOETHE

Giving advice isn't as risky as people say. Few ever take it anyway. WILLIAM FEATHER

Never give advice in a crowd. ARAB PROVERB

We may give advice but we cannot give conduct.
BENJAMIN FRANKLIN

I always advise people never to give advice.
P. G. WODEHOUSE

ACTING

Read all the Shakespeare you can; if you can play Shakespeare, you can play anything.
JOHN CARRADINE

First wipe your nose and check your flies.
ALEC GUINNESS

Never get caught acting.   LILLIAN GISH

If *you* cried a little less, the audience would cry more.
EDITH EVANS to John Gielgud

Have a very good reason for everything you do.
LAURENCE OLIVIER

Play well, or play badly, but play truly.
STANISLAVSKY

Know your lines and don't bump into the furniture.
SPENCER TRACY

Whatever you do kid, always serve it with a little dressing.
GEORGE M. COHAN TO SPENCER TRACY

Use your weaknesses; aspire to the strength.
LAURENCE OLIVIER

Pray to God and say the lines.   BETTE DAVIS

Pick up your cues and piss off.   NOEL COWARD

Act in your pauses.   ELLEN TERRY to Cedric Hardwicke

If you want to help the American theater, don't
be an actress, be an audience.
TALLULAH BANKHEAD

When you go into the professional world, at a
stock theater somewhere, backstage you will meet
an older actor—someone who has been around
awhile. He will tell you tales and anecdotes about
life in the theater. He will speak to you about
your performance and the performances of oth-

ers, and he will generalize to you, based on his experience and his intuitions, about the laws of the stage. Ignore this man.   SANFORD MEISNER

○-○

A young Clark Gable took Louis B. Mayer's advice to have all his teeth pulled—merely because Mayer felt that false teeth would "look better" on the screen.

○-○

Don't think you're funny. It'll never work if you think you're funny.
        GEORGE ABBOTT to an actor in a comic role

        To be a character who feels a deep emotion, one must go into the memory's vault and mix in a sad memory from one's own life.   ALBERT FINNEY

Nobody "becomes" a character. You can't act unless you are who you are.   MARLON BRANDO

        You have to work years in hit shows to make people sick and tired of you, but you can accomplish this in a few weeks on television.
                                WALTER SLEZAK

○-○

KEVIN KLINE: (upon being introduced to John Gielgud) Mr. Gielgud, have you any advice for a young actor about to make his first film in London?
JOHN GIELGUD: The really good restaurants are in Chelsea and the outlying regions—you want to avoid the restaurants in the big hotels.

○-○

My advice to actresses is don't worry about your looks. The very thing that makes you unhappy in your appearance may be the one thing to make you a star.   ESTELLE WINWOOD

○-○

Don't be afraid to be outrageous; the critics will shoot you down anyway.   LAURENCE OLIVIER to Anthony Hopkins

○-○

The important thing in acting is to be able to laugh and cry. If I have to cry, I think of my sex life. If I have to laugh, I think of my sex life.
                                        GLENDA JACKSON

Talk low, talk slow, and don't say too much.

JOHN WAYNE

Don't act, think.   DAVID LEAN

∘-∘

In future, when you want to put something into your part
that is not in the play, you must ask the author—or some
other author—to lead up to the interpolation for you.
Never forget that the effect of a line may depend not on
its delivery, but on something said earlier in the play
either by somebody else or by yourself, and that if you
change it it my be necessary to change the whole first act
as well. Now, I can't rewrite *Joan* for you, though it would
be great fun.   GEORGE BERNARD SHAW to Wendy Hiller

∘-∘

If you achieve success, you will get applause.
Enjoy it—but never quite believe it.

ROBERT MONTGOMERY

Don't use your conscious past, use your creative
imagination to create a past that belongs to your
character. I don't want you to be stuck with your
own life. It's too little! It's too bitty-caca.

STELLA ADLER

Your motivation is your pay packet on Friday. Now get on with it.
NOEL COWARD

Ingrid Bergman told her director, Alfred Hitchcock, that she just could not play a certain scene "naturally." "Then *fake* it," Hitchcock advised.

It is a great help for a man to be in love with himself. For an actor, however, it is absolutely essential.   ROBERT MORLEY

Just let the wardrobe do the acting.
                    JACK NICHOLSON to Michael Keaton,
                              on the set of *Batman*

The first thing you should do when you win an Oscar is thank God. The second thing you should do is forget it. The third thing you should do is call your agent and tell him you need a job.
                                        ROD STEIGER

Use a make-up table with everything close at hand and don't rush; otherwise you'll look like a patchwork quilt.   LUCILLE BALL

Never take top billing. You'll last longer that way.
BING CROSBY

o-o-o-o-o-o-o-o-o-o-o-o-o-o-o-o-o-o-o-o-o-o-o-o-o-o-o-o-o-o-o-o-o-o-o-o-o-o-o-o

The one word you'll need is *no*.
BETTE DAVIS to Robin Williams

o-o-o-o-o-o-o-o-o-o-o-o-o-o-o-o-o-o-o-o-o-o-o-o-o-o-o-o-o-o-o-o-o-o-o-o-o-o-o-o

The most important thing in acting is honesty. If you can fake that, you've got it made.
GEORGE BURNS

o-o-o-o-o-o-o-o-o-o-o-o-o-o-o-o-o-o-o-o-o-o-o-o-o-o-o-o-o-o-o-o-o-o-o-o-o-o-o-o

After Norma Talmadge's performance as Madame Du Barry in *Woman of Passion* (1930) was a critical and box office disaster, her sister Constance wired the following advice: LEAVE THEM WHILE YOU'RE LOOKING GOOD AND THANK GOD FOR THE TRUST FUNDS MOMMA SET UP.

o-o-o-o-o-o-o-o-o-o-o-o-o-o-o-o-o-o-o-o-o-o-o-o-o-o-o-o-o-o-o-o-o-o-o-o-o-o-o-o

Actors should be overheard, not listened to, and the audience is fifty percent of the performance.
SHIRLEY BOOTH

Lead the audience by the nose to the thought.
LAURENCE OLIVIER

You're at a level where you can only afford one mistake. The higher up you go, the more mistakes you're allowed. Right at the top, if you make enough of them, it's considered to be your style.   FRED ASTAIRE to Jack Lemmon

If you're going to make rubbish, be the best rubbish in it.   RICHARD BURTON

Don't get a college degree. You don't need it in the theater. It's a waste of four years. Go to New York (or L.A.), where the work is. Take acting classes, dance classes, singing, fencing, improvisation, etc. Hang out with other young people who are serious about getting into the business. Audition for everything, even if you don't stand a chance. Activity breeds activity. Getting a college education so you'll have something to fall back on if things don't work out, which your parents and other sensible people will urge you to do, means you're not convinced you're invincible. Only people who believe they're invincible stand a chance of making it in show business. Even if it occurs to you as a *possibility* that you won't "make it," then you won't. (This advice is null and void if you happen to get into Yale Drama School, which makes you part of the clique that spawned Meryl Streep, William Hurt, and Sigourney Weaver.)

ORSON BEAN

<hr>

Soon after Ralph Bellamy arrived in Hollywood on the Santa Fe Chief to shoot his first picture, his co-star Clark Gable gave him this advice: "I just got $11,000 for playing a heavy in a western. $11,000! No actor is worth that much. I got myself a cheap room and a second-hand Ford and I'm not buying anything you can't put on the Chief because this ain't going to last. Never buy anything you can't put on the Chief."

<hr>

Walk in, plant yourself, look the other fellow in the eye, and tell the truth.   JAMES CAGNEY

The best research [for playing drunk] is being a British actor for twenty years.   MICHAEL CAINE

Stick to your inkpots, kid, actors don't eat regularly.
ANONYMOUS colleague advising cartoonist
Milton Caniff to avoid the stage.

o-o-o-o-o-o-o-o-o-o-o-o-o-o-o-o-o-o-o-o-o-o-o-o-o-o-o-o-o-o-o-o-o-o-o-o-o

I'm afraid you'll never make it as an actor. But as a star, I think you might well hit the jackpot.

ORSON WELLES to Joseph Cotten

o-o-o-o-o-o-o-o-o-o-o-o-o-o-o-o-o-o-o-o-o-o-o-o-o-o-o-o-o-o-o-o-o-o-o-o-o

What acting means is that you've got to get out of your own skin.   KATHARINE HEPBURN

o-o-o-o-o-o-o-o-o-o-o-o-o-o-o-o-o-o-o-o-o-o-o-o-o-o-o-o-o-o-o-o-o-o-o-o-o

You'll never make it as a juggler, m'boy. Your eyes are too sad. But don't listen to me, kid. My entire success is based on one rule: never take advice from anybody!

W. C. FIELDS to Paul Muni

o-o-o-o-o-o-o-o-o-o-o-o-o-o-o-o-o-o-o-o-o-o-o-o-o-o-o-o-o-o-o-o-o-o-o-o-o

People disappoint you. Lovers disappoint you. But theatrical memorabilia stays with you, as long as you keep it under clear plastic.

SYLVIA MILES

AGEING

Growing old is no more than a bad habit which a busy person has no time to form.

ANDRÉ MAUROIS

You can't help getting older, but you don't have to get old.

GEORGE BURNS

You can't turn back the clock. But you can wind it up again.

BONNIE PRUDDEN

One should never make one's debut with a scandal. One should reserve that to give an interest to one's old age.

OSCAR WILDE

The first sign of age . . . is when you go out into the streets . . . and recognize for the first time how young the policemen look.

SEYMOUR HICKS

Remember that as a teenager you are in the last stage of your life when you will be happy to hear that the phone is for you.

FRAN LEBOWITZ

The trick is growing up without growing old.
CASEY STENGEL

The answer to old age is to keep one's mind busy
and to go on with one's life as if it were intermi-
nable. I always admired Chekhov for building a
new house when he was dying of tuberculosis.
LEON EDEL

Stay busy, get plenty of exercise, and don't drink
too much. Then again, don't drink too little.
HERMAN "JACKRABBIT" SMITH-JOHANNSEN

If you want to stay young-looking, pick your parents very carefully. DICK CLARK

Age is a question of mind over matter. If you
don't mind, it doesn't matter. SATCHEL PAIGE

When you get older you have to be careful about
always saying, "Things aren't as good as they
used to be." But it's hard not to. ANDY ROONEY

You're never too old to become younger.
MAE WEST

○-○

THE 2,000-YEAR-OLD MAN'S
SECRETS OF LONGEVITY

1. Don't run for a bus—there'll always be another.
2. Never, ever touch fried food.
3. Stay out of a Ferrari or any other small Italian car.
4. Eat fruit—a nectarine—even a rotten plum is good.

MEL BROOKS

○-○

No one is ever old enough to know better.

HOLBROOK JACKSON

When you get past fifty, you have to decide
whether to keep your face or your figure. I kept
my face.   BARBARA CARTLAND

Nature gives you the face you have at twenty,
but it's up to you to merit the face you have at fifty.

COCO CHANEL

I'll tell ya how to stay young: Hang around with
older people.   BOB HOPE

The denunciation of the young is a necessary part of the hygiene of older people, and greatly assists the circulation of the blood.

LOGAN PEARSALL SMITH

The secret of staying young is to live honestly, eat slowly, and lie about your age.

LUCILLE BALL

ALWAYS . . .

Always be a little kinder than necessary.
JAMES M. BARRIE

Always let your flattery be seen through, for what really flatters a man is that you think him worth flattering.
GEORGE BERNARD SHAW

Always do sober what you said you'd do drunk. That will teach you to keep your mouth shut.
ERNEST HEMINGWAY

Always rise from the table with an appetite, and you will never sit down without one.
WILLIAM PENN

One should always play fairly when one has the winning cards.
OSCAR WILDE

Always live in the ugliest house on the street— then you don't have to look at it.
DAVID HOCKNEY

Murder is always a mistake. . . . One should never
do anything that one cannot talk about after dinner.
OSCAR WILDE

It is always the best policy to tell the truth, unless, of course, you are an exceptionally good liar.
JEROME K. JEROME

Therefore, from a logical point of view,
Always marry a woman uglier than you.
CALYPSO SONG

Always fornicate between clean sheets and spit
on a well-scrubbed floor.   CHRISTOPHER FRY

Always treat a lady like a whore, and a whore
like a lady.   WILSON MIZNER

Always forgive your enemies—nothing annoys
them so much.   OSCAR WILDE

Always make water when you can.
DUKE OF WELLINGTON

There are many things to be remembered when making friends with the animals in the zoo. In the first place they dislike gloves, and a gloved hand is far more likely to be bitten than a naked one.

HELEN M. SIDEBOTHAM

If a ferret bites you it is nearly always your own fault.

PHIL DRABBLE

Before a cat will condescend
To treat you as a trusted friend,
Some little token of esteem
Is needed, like a dish of cream.

T. S. ELIOT

○-○

Dorothy Parker's advice to a friend whose ailing cat had to be put down: "Try curiosity."

○-○

Cats with blue eyes are invariably deaf.

CHARLES DARWIN

The cat who doesn't act finicky soon loses control of his owner.   "MORRIS THE CAT"

Take a dog for a companion and a stick in your hand.   ENGLISH PROVERB

If you pick up a starving dog and make him prosperous, he will not bite you. This is the principal difference between a dog and a man.
    MARK TWAIN

The best way to get a puppy is to beg for a baby brother—and they'll settle for a puppy every time.
    WINSTON PENDELTON

Dachshunds are ideal dogs for small children, as they are already stretched and pulled to such a length that the child cannot do much harm one way or the other.   ROBERT BENCHLEY

Don't make the mistake of treating your dogs like humans, or they'll treat you like dogs.
    MARTHA SCOTT

Money will buy a pretty good dog, but it won't buy the wag of his tail.   JOSH BILLINGS

Anyone who is concerned about his dignity would be well advised to keep away from horses.

DUKE OF EDINBURGH

You cannot keep a fully grown chimpanzee in the house. If he decides to throw himself at you out of affection he can easily knock you down the stairs. They also become unpredictable and lose their tempers for no apparent reason, and are capable of causing considerable damage around the house.

TERRY MURPHY

The elephant is never won with anger.

EARL OF ROCHESTER

He who drives fat oxen should himself be fat.

SAMUEL JOHNSON

You cannot shoot an animal twice—but you *can* photograph it twice.

JOHN MAUDE

It does not matter how badly you paint so long as you don't paint badly like other people.

GEORGE MOORE

You've the stuff, old kid—all you have to do is keep it up.

THOMAS HART BENTON to Jackson Pollock

It is the eye of ignorance that assigns a fixed and unchangeable color to every object; beware of this stumbling block.   PAUL GAUGUIN

Artists can color the sky red because they know it's blue. Those of us who aren't artists must color things the way they really are or people might think we're stupid.   JULES FEIFFER

An artist should be fit for the best society and keep out of it.   JOHN RUSKIN

Painting is easy when you don't know how, but very difficult when you do.   EDGAR DEGAS

The rule in the art world is: you cater to the masses or you kowtow to the elite; you can't have both.   BEN HECHT

Nobody can count themselves an artist unless they can carry a picture in their head before they paint it.   CLAUDE MONET

The artist who aims at perfection in everything achieves it in nothing.   EUGÈNE DELACROIX

It is a good idea, particularly when you are doing the eyes, to get the sitter to look at you. In this way the portrait will look in every direction and at everyone who looks at it. This is something much praised by those who do not understand how it is done.   ANTONIO PALOMINO Y VELASCO

When I did my self-portrait, I left all the pimples out because you always should. Pimples are a temporary condition and they don't have anything to do with what you really look like. Always omit the blemishes—they're not part of the good picture you want.   ANDY WARHOL

It is a mistake for a sculptor or a painter to speak or write very often about his job. It releases tension needed for his work.   HENRY MOORE

Whoever wishes to devote himself to painting should begin by cutting out his own tongue.
                                                    HENRI MATISSE

You study, you learn, but you guard the original naiveté. It has to be within you, as desire for drink is within the drunkard or love is within the lover.   HENRI MATISSE

Immature artists imitate. Mature artists steal.
                                                    LIONEL TRILLING

You have to hang on in periods when your style isn't popular, because if it's good, it'll come back, and you'll be a recognized beauty once again.
                                                    ANDY WARHOL

Never put more than two waves in a picture; it's fussy.   WINSLOW HOMER

Pictures must not be too picturesque.

RALPH WALDO EMERSON

If you can't find your inspiration by walking around the block one time, go around two blocks—but never three.

ROBERT MOTHERWELL

Art is a collaboration between God and the artist, and the less the artist does the better.

ANDRÉ GIDE

Nothing can be rushed. Things must grow, they must grow upward . . .

PAUL KLEE

Have no fear of perfection—you'll never reach it.

SALVADOR DALI

o-o-o-o-o-o-o-o-o-o-o-o-o-o-o-o-o-o-o-o-o-o-o-o-o-o-o-o-o-o-o-o-o-o-o-o

Bob [Rauschenberg] knocked on the door to my studio one day, and brought in a painting he had just finished. It was a new one in the black series. I think he felt my reaction to it was not sufficiently enthusiastic. I had been very enthusiastic about his work, and he may have felt I was disappointed. In any case, I suddenly realized that he was terribly upset, close to tears. Well, I gave him a good talking-to about that. I told him he simply could not be dependent on anyone's opinion, that he could never, never look to another person for that sort of support.

JOHN CAGE

∘-∘

It is very good advice to believe only what an artist does, rather than what he says about his work. DAVID HOCKNEY

Three things are needed for success in painting and sculpture: to see beauty when young and accustom oneself to it, to work hard, and to obtain good advice. GIANLORENZO BERNINI

Very few people possess true artistic ability. It is therefore both unseemly and unproductive to irritate the situation by making an effort. If you have a burning, restless urge to write or paint, simply eat something sweet and the feeling will pass. FRAN LEBOWITZ

BASEBALL

Throw high risers at the chin; throw peas at the knees; throw it here when they're lookin' there; throw it there when they're lookin' here.

SATCHEL PAIGE

The game is supposed to be fun. If you have a bad day, don't worry about it. You can't expect to get a hit every game.   YOGI BERRA

Bring all you got.   BOB GIBSON

Have fun.   JIM BOUTON

Throw strikes. Home plate don't move.

SATCHEL PAIGE

Keep your eye clear and hit 'em where they ain't.

WEE WILLIE KEELER

Swing at the strikes.   YOGI BERRA

Don't forget to swing hard, in case you hit the ball.   WOODIE HELD

There are two theories on hitting the knuckleball. Unfortunately, neither of them works.

CHARLIE LAU

The way to catch a knuckleball is to wait until the ball stops rolling and then pick it up.

BOB UECKER

If they try to knock you over, hit the motherfucker right in the mouth with the ball. BILLY MARTIN

A catcher and his body are like an outlaw and his horse: You've got to ride that nag 'til it drops.

JOHNNY BENCH

Never trust a base runner who's limping. Comes a base hit and you'll think he just got back from Lourdes. JOE GARAGIOLA

Don't park in the spaces marked, "Reserved for Umpires." JOHN MCSHERRY

o-o-o-o-o-o-o-o-o-o-o-o-o-o-o-o-o-o-o-o-o-o-o-o-o-o-o-o-o-o-o-o-o-o-o

When I first became a manager, I asked Chuck [Tanner] for advice. He told me, "Always rent."   TONY LARUSSA

o-o-o-o-o-o-o-o-o-o-o-o-o-o-o-o-o-o-o-o-o-o-o-o-o-o-o-o-o-o-o-o-o-o-o

The secret of managing is to keep the guys who hate you away from the guys who are undecided.
CASEY STENGEL

Get yourself a coach to drink with or else you'll go nuts.   JIM FREGOSI

You gotta lose 'em sometime. When you do, lose 'em right.   CASEY STENGEL

You must have an alibi to show why you lost. If you haven't one, you must fake one. Your self-confidence must be maintained.
CHRISTY MATHEWSON

Kids should practice autographing baseballs. This is a skill that's often overlooked in Little League.
TUG MCGRAW

THE BEST ADVICE I'VE EVER RECEIVED

The best piece of advice was not to be an actress.
ISABELLA ROSSELLINI

There are two kinds of worries—those you can do something about and those you can't. Don't spend any time on the latter.
NAT HENTOFF (from Duke Ellington)

Show me a guy who's afraid to look bad, and I'll show you a guy you can beat every time.
RENÉ AUBERJONOIS (from Lou Brock)

Go west, old man.
IRVING "SWIFTY" LAZAR (from Moss Hart)

If someone says "can't," that shows you what to do.
JOHN CAGE (from his father)

I had no desire to be involved in the music business, but I saw that Jerry Brandt, who was the head of the music department at William Morris, had a limousine, and he was hanging out with Mick Jagger. I asked him, "Jerry, how do you get a limo?" He said, "Schmuck, you're twenty-four years old. Do you think Norman Jewison is going to sign with you? Does Irene Dunne want you to be her agent? You better get into the music business with people your own age." I thought that was the best advice I'd ever heard, and that's how I got into the music business.

DAVID GEFFEN

Never tell a woman that you didn't realize she was pregnant unless you're certain that she *is*.

DAVE BARRY

Pay no attention to whatever advice you receive.

EDWARD GOREY

To marry the girl I did. And *she* gave me the advice. GENERAL MARK CLARK

Friendship cannot be negotiated.

PAUL KRASSNER (from Lyle Stuart)

The best advice I ever received was to buy Berkshire Hathaway (now $5,000 a share) at $300. Unfortunately, I ignored it. Other good advice I have all too often ignored: know your audience, be prepared, don't pretend to know something if you don't, try to know *something,* don't bite off more than you can chew, don't chew with your mouth open, never wear brown suits, avoid fat in your diet, avoid giving other people advice.

ANDREW TOBIAS

Always pee before a long car trip.

MARTIN MULL

Don't fight the problem, decide it.

GENERAL GEORGE C. MARSHALL

Never give advice—it will just backfire on you.

FATHER GUIDO SARDUCCI (DON NOVELLO)

The advice that means the most to me right now was not delivered directly to me. It's something I read that Fred Astaire said about his dance routines: "Get it 'til it's perfect, then cut two minutes."

SUSAN STAMBERG

The best advice I've ever received was the one tangible piece of broadcasting education I received while attending Cornell. One of my professors, the general manager of a local radio station, advised me as follows: "Always address the audience as one person. Whenever I hear someone say, 'Hello again, everyone,' or 'Good morning, world,' I always look around to see who's come into the room with me."   KEITH OLBERMANN

If you can pick it up or drink it in one sitting, take it.

> JAMES SRODES (from Horace G. "Buddy" Davis, Jr., 1971 Pulitzer Prize winner for editorial writing and journalism professor —on the permissible limits of graft by reporters)

> The late Dick Gordon, a.k.a. "The Fox," the sports information director at Hofstra College when I was an undergraduate, thought I was not tough enough to be a journalist. He once told me, "Spike"—he called a lot of people Spike—"you'd better become a schoolteacher." That made me mad, but he also got me a job at *Newsday*, and I vowed to show him he was wrong.
>
> GEORGE VECSEY

Don't eat yellow snow.   W. P. KINSELLA

I once complained to my father that I didn't seem to be able to do things the same way other people did. Dad's advice? "Margo, don't be a sheep. People hate sheep. They eat sheep."

MARGO KAUFMAN

The best advice I ever received was not to try to crash in at the top. Announcer Milton Cross suggested I not audition at ABC New York (I was eighteen years old), but put in some time with small stations and get the kind of experience that might make a big network want me. He was right, even though I didn't comprehend it at the time.

HUGH DOWNS

Don't mourn, organize.

PETE SEEGER (from Joe Hill)

My high school English teacher at the Bronx High School of Science, Dr. Isobel Gordon, used to deal with smart but lazy students who were trying to coast through her classes by telling us: "Don't *smell* the poem—*read* it!" In other words, don't slide by; dig in and reach for the best you've got.

JEFF GREENFIELD

The best advice I ever received was from my composition teacher, Darius Milhaud. He told me that I had come to him too late to develop as a schooled musician in European classical tradition. But, he said, I possessed something unique which I should not set aside; instead, [I should] apply my knowledge of jazz to composition and I would successfully reflect my own American culture. Rather than deny that which was part of my native background, he urged me to cultivate it. In other words, he applied to music the same lesson that Socrates taught long ago: "Know thyself. And to one's own self be true."   DAVE BRUBECK

From my father: "Always be ready to come off the bench." It was his way of saying, "Be prepared."   MORTON DEAN

Save your money.   PHYLLIS DILLER

If you want to be a writer—stop talking about it and sit down and write!   JACKIE COLLINS

The best advice I've ever received was from my first editor, Paul C. Smith, as I began my column

in July 1938: "For god's sake, kid, be entertaining. And remember, I have a short attention span."
HERB CAEN

"Take a chance—Columbus did."   BUD COLLINS
(from his mother)

The best advice I ever received was back in 1958 when I was playing the piano in a bar on Capitol Hill in Washington, D.C. A congressman came up to me and said, "Kid, stop singing 'Stardust' and start singing about Congress. We are funny. Pay attention to us and you will have a brand-new career." I never got to thank him. He was indicted shortly after that.   MARK RUSSELL

Mark Twain to young writers: "Whatever you like best, strike it out."   THOMAS BOSWELL

○-○

I don't recall ever receiving any explicit advice. No Horace Greeley ever told me to go west, young man. And I could have used a Polonius or two. Even an Ann Landers. Advice in real life is hard to come by. People who give it are either too free with it or want too much money.

Television, however, is both free, and free with advice: "Lying is wrong, Barney, you see that now, don't you?" or "Don't try to be something you're not," or "You're half-human, Spock. Always remember that." Children's programming, in particular, seethes with advice: Hold somebody's hand when you cross the street; hug, don't hit; sharing is caring; etc. Children tolerate this secular humanist preaching, but I suspect they would rather watch Road Runner cartoons because they have no message at all, or rather they have a dark message: you can try to get what you want, Coyote, but you'll never get it, and you'll get hurt bad trying. This message is not uplifting, but it seems true to me.

My parents frequently offered implicit advice. My mother, especially, had a way of saying, "Oh, for Pete's sake," which held a variety of meanings, depending on the context of the utterance. It could mean, "You should clean your room now," or "I think it would be a good idea if you got a job," or even, "Go west, young man, the sooner the better."

A couple years back, I did get advice of a sort from a television producer. I was among the cast of a comedy special, and we were about to tape before a live audience. The producer told us, "Don't get too hung up on the acting. Go for the laughs." I don't know how this holds up as advice, but if you substitute "responsibility" for "the acting," and "money" for "laughs," it does seem to form a pretty good metaphor for the Reagan era.

MERLE KESSLER (A.K.A. IAN SHOALES)

From Hemingway: Develop a built-in bullshit detector. STANLEY KARNOW

The best advice I've ever received is the advice I have for young broadcasters: "The best way to sound like you know what you're talking about is to know what you're talking about." But young broadcasters rarely ask for advice. "How did you get your job? How much money do you make?" —that's what they want to know. SCOTT SIMON

If you want to do it, do it!

FRANCESCO SCAVULLO (from his father)

My grandfather told me that there are no free rides in this world. This is why I do not take federal grants of funding for Westside Preparatory School. He also told me to be all that I could be. I repeat these words to myself each day be-

fore beginning my day, "Be all that you can
be . . ."   MARVA COLLINS

When I was a young newspaperman, an old, gray-
haired sportswriter named Harry Grayson said to
me: "Always remember: when you freeload, bitch.
You maintain dignity."   IRA BERKOW

Never open your own restaurant.
                                                PIERRE FRANEY

                        Take the cash. JOE QUEENAN

You don't know what's going on.
                                                DUANE MICHALS

The best advice I ever received was from my
co-author of *You Can't Afford the Luxury of a
Negative Thought,* John-Roger, who once told
me, "You can have anything you want. You just
can't have everything you want."
                                                PETER MCWILLIAMS

Trust your instincts. If you have no instincts,
trust your impulses.
                        TAMMY GRIMES (from Noel Coward)

My father told me when I was writing *Russian Blood,* three things to bear in mind: 1. Is it true? 2. Is it kind? 3. Is it necessary?

ALEX SHOUMATOFF

"Young man, never be a solemn ass."
TOM WICKER (from Jonathan Daniels)

The best advice I have ever received was given to me by the late journalist Damon Runyon: "Get as mad as you like but never get off the payroll."
DAVID BROWN

I've never gotten any good advice. I've had to figure everything out for myself.

TOM MAGLIOZZI

A. "Be sure you're right, then go ahead." (from Davy Crockett on my eighth birthday)
B. "Rome wasn't built in a day." (from Burton Zucker upon leaving Milwaukee for L.A.)
C. "Buy a tuxedo." (from Howard W. Koch after the premiere of *Airplane!*) DAVID ZUCKER

The best advice I've ever received? How about the strangest? When I was thirteen, my father took me aside and told me that all a girl needed to know to get by in life was written on the top of a mayonnaise jar. I puzzled for days about the meaning of the phrase, "Refrigerate After Opening" —until my father remarked that in his day mayo jars always said, "Keep Cool, Don't Freeze."

C. E. CRIMMINS

Perhaps one of the only positive pieces of advice that I was ever given was that supplied by an old courtier who observed: "Only two rules really count: never miss an opportunity to relieve yourself; never miss a chance to rest your feet."

DUKE OF WINDSOR

o-o-o-o-o-o-o-o-o-o-o-o-o-o-o-o-o-o-o-o-o o o-o-o-o-o-o-o-o-o-o-o-o-o

What's the best advice I've ever received? Many nuggets, proffered at many stages of my life. When I was a thirteen-year-old, having run away from home, in 1947, I chanced to spend a night in company with a group of "Gentlemen of the Road," what used to be called hobos before Reagan got pricey with such terms as "the homeless" or "the underclasses." They were kind to a footloose kid, and they shared their dinner with me. That was the first time I ever drank "hobo coffee," and the old man who was brewing it in a quart tin can advised me, "Son, you wanna take the bitter outta the joe, you scrape clean the shells of a coupla eggs, and put'm them shells in the water. Pinch of salt don't hurt none, neither." That may have been the first best advice I've ever received.

The next one was from the first woman who ever deigned to favor me with sex. She says she'll sue me if I use her name, but she cannot much mind if I pass on the wisdom she imparted as we struggled on the sofa in my mother's apartment in Cleveland: "Do you have a rubber? Don't *ever* go to bed with a girl if you aren't wearing a rubber." This simple wisdom has come full circle, back into the garden-variety common sense, though I took it as gospel then and for many years thereafter till I assumed the responsibility fully in 1975 when I had my vasectomy.

Though he hated me, my first sergeant during Ranger basic at Fort Benning in 1957, one Bedzyk by name, inadvertently gave me a chunk of change that saved me grief in later years by telling me, "Don't get shot, because there ain't no such thing as a 'flesh wound' like in the cowboy pictures. They hit you anywhere, the shock'll probably kill you." In none of my stories do the private detectives suffer gunshot wounds without taking a dive and spending some chapters in Intensive.

When I got to Hollywood, I received three pieces of advice that have guided my actions in all dealings with producers and studios and networks. The first was from the late Howard Rodman, a great writer and a superb, ethical human being. He said: "If they want to fuck around with your words, don't let them lie to you and con you or seduce you, and don't let them send you to lawyers. If they want to change your words . . . *hit them*!" (To this day, there are whole networks where I'm not allowed to work.)

The other two bits of smart came from the late Charles Beaumont, another extraordinary talent, who said on my first night in Hollywood, as we shot pool in a joint in the Valley, "Achieving success in this town is like climbing a gigantic mountain of cow flop just so you can pluck one perfect rose from the top. And you find, after having made that hideous ascent, that you have lost the sense of smell." Later that night he said: "Don't stop writing books and stories. The minute you do nothing but screenplays, they consider you one of their whores. They think books are magic, and they treat someone who can do them well as a Prince from a Far Land." HARLAN ELLISON

o-o-o-o-o-o-o-o-o-o-o-o-o-o-o-o-o-o-o-o-o-o-o-o-o-o-o-o-o-o-o-o-o-o-o-o-o

BUSINESS

Beware of all enterprises that require new clothes.
THOREAU

Be careful, and you will save many men from the sin of robbing you.
ED HOWE

The secret of business is to know something that nobody else knows.
ARISTOTLE ONASSIS

Don't do anything you wouldn't be willing to explain on television.
ARJAY MILLER

∞∞∞∞∞∞∞∞∞∞∞∞∞∞∞∞∞∞∞∞∞∞∞∞∞∞∞∞∞∞∞∞

Dear, never forget one little point: It's my business. You just work here.
ELIZABETH ARDEN to her husband

∞∞∞∞∞∞∞∞∞∞∞∞∞∞∞∞∞∞∞∞∞∞∞∞∞∞∞∞∞∞∞∞

Call upon a man of business during hours of business only to transact your business. Then go about your business and give him time to attend to his business.
ANONYMOUS

> Whenever you're sitting across from some important person, always picture him sitting there in a suit of long underwear. That's the way I always operated in business. JOSEPH P. KENNEDY

You can fool all the people all the time if the advertising is right and the budget is big enough.
JOSEPH E. LEVINE

> As to the idea that advertising motivates people, remember the Edsel. PETER DRUCKER

A verbal contract isn't worth the paper it's written on. LOUIS B. MAYER

The department-store heir Alfred Bloomingdale loved musical comedies and backed a number of Broadway productions, all unsuccessfully. Undeterred by the series of flops, he invested a large sum in a turkey called *Allah Be Praised*. During the disastrous tryout in Boston, Bloomingdale engaged a noted play doctor named Cy Howard who, after sitting through the entire show in silence, finally turned to Bloomingdale and advised, "Al, close the show and keep the store open at night."

Having served on various committees, I have drawn up a list of rules: Never arrive on time; this stamps you as a beginner. Don't say anything until the meeting is half over; this stamps you as wise. Be as vague as possible; this avoids irritating the others. When in doubt, suggest a subcommittee be appointed. Be the first to move for adjournment; this will make you popular; it's what everyone is waiting for. HARRY CHAPMAN

If you see a snake, just kill it—don't appoint a committee on snakes. H. ROSS PEROT

Make three correct guesses consecutively and you will establish a reputation as an expert.
LAURENCE J. PETER

Don't steal; thou'lt never thus compete successfully in business. Cheat. AMBROSE BIERCE

The customer's always right.
The son-of-a-bitch
Is probably rich
So smile with all your might.
NOEL COWARD

Don't go to business school.
PAUL HAWKEN to aspiring entrepreneurs

Punctuality is one of the cardinal business virtues: always insist on it in your subordinates.
DON MARQUIS

Think big, be big.
BARRY MINKOW, former ZZZZ Best "Carpet King," now serving a twenty-year prison sentence for securities fraud, conspiracy, and money laundering

Beware of the man who will not engage in idle conversation; he is planning to steal your walking stick or water your stock.   WILLIAM EMERSON

All business sagacity reduces itself in the last analysis to a judicious use of sabotage.
THORSTEIN VEBLEN

A businessman needs three umbrellas—one to leave at the office, one to leave at home, and one to leave on the train.   PAUL DICKSON

○-○

Don't be a salary slave! If you are going to do anything in this world, you must start before you are forty, before your period of initiative has ended. Do it now!

> ROBERT COCHRANE, a Chicago advertising executive, to Carl Laemmle, who took the advice, quit his job as a clothing store manager, and eventually became a movie mogul

○-○

It is very vulgar to talk about one's own business. Only people like stockbrokers do that, and then merely at dinner parties. OSCAR WILDE

> If you don't do it excellently, don't do it at all. Because if it's not excellent, it won't be profitable or fun, and if you're not in business for fun or profit, what the hell are you doing there?
>
> ROBERT TOWNSEND

If you have too many problems, maybe you should go out of business. There is no law that says a company must last forever. PETER DRUCKER

> Mind your own business. CERVANTES

CHILDREN

It sometimes happens, even in the best of families, that a baby is born. This is not necessarily cause for alarm. The important thing is to keep your wits about you and borrow some money.
ELINOR GOULDING SMITH

One of the most important things to remember about infant care is: never change diapers in midstream.
DON MARQUIS

Do not videotape your child in the bathtub. Do not name your child after a Scandinavian deity or any aspect of the weather.
DANIEL MENAKER

To be a successful father there's one absolute rule: when you have a kid, don't look at it for the first two years.
ERNEST HEMINGWAY

When you strike a child, take care that you strike it in anger, even at the risk of maiming it for life. A blow in cold blood neither can nor should be forgiven.
GEORGE BERNARD SHAW

If a child shows himself incorrigible, he should be decently and quietly beheaded at the age of twelve.
DON MARQUIS

A child hasn't a grown-up person's appetite for affection. A little of it goes a long way with them; and they like a good imitation of it better than the real thing, as every nurse knows.
GEORGE BERNARD SHAW

The secret of dealing successfully with a child is not to be its parent.
MELL LAZARUS

The best way to keep children at home is to make the home atmosphere pleasant, and let the air out of the tires.
DOROTHY PARKER

Your responsibility as a parent is not as great as you might imagine. You need not supply the world with the next conqueror of disease or major motion picture star. If your child simply grows up to be someone who does not use the word "collectible" as a noun, you can consider yourself an unqualified success.
FRAN LEBOWITZ

Getting down on all fours and imitating a rhinoceros stops babies from crying. (Put an empty cigarette pack on your nose for a horn and make loud "snort" noises.) I don't know why parents don't do this more often. Usually it makes the kid laugh. Sometimes it sends him into shock. Either way it quiets him down. If you're a parent, acting like a rhino has another advantage. Keep it up until the kid is a teenager and he definitely won't have his friends hanging around your house all the time.   P. J. O'ROURKE

If you treat a sick child like an adult and a sick adult like a child, everything usually works out pretty well.   RUTH CARLISLE

God knows that a mother needs fortitude and courage and tolerance and flexibility and patience and firmness and nearly every other brave aspect of the human soul. But because I happen to be a parent of almost fiercely maternal nature, I praise *casualness*. It seems to me the rarest of virtues. It is useful enough when children are small. It is important to the point of necessity when they are adolescents.   PHYLLIS McGINLEY

A food is not necessarily essential just because your child hates it.   KATHERINE WHITEHORN

Ask your child what he wants for dinner only if he's buying.   FRAN LEBOWITZ

If you must hold yourself up to your children as an object lesson, hold yourself up as a warning and not as an example. GEORGE BERNARD SHAW

Any college that would take your son he should be too proud to go to.   ERMA BOMBECK

The best sex education for kids is when Daddy pats Mommy on the fanny when he comes home from work.   DR. WILLIAM H. MASTERS

Even very young children need to be informed about dying. Explain the concept of death very carefully to your child. This will make threatening him with it much more effective.

P. J. O'ROURKE

Never allow your child to call you by your first name. He hasn't known you long enough.

FRAN LEBOWITZ

The real menace in dealing with a five-year-old is that in no time at all you begin to sound like a five-year-old.   JEAN KERR

Do your kids a favor—don't have any.
                                   ROBERT ORBEN

DIRECTING

As soon as you have chosen a subject for a film, you have already made a success or a failure.

BILLY WILDER

If you are a young director, or wish to be, the number one thing you've got to have is a screenplay. You can't win your millions on the roulette table unless you've got a chip to put on the numbers—and your chip in the film business is a script.

MICHAEL WINNER

You have to accept that the movie isn't going to be as good as you wanted it to be.

DAVID LEAN

The more successful the villain, the more successful the picture.

ALFRED HITCHCOCK

Three or four good effective scenes is enough to make a picture interesting. That's all you want.

LASLO BENEDEK

Occasionally you get some luck in pictures. More occasionally you have bad luck. If something happens that wasn't premeditated, photograph it.

JOHN FORD

If you cast wrong, you are in a lot of trouble.
PAUL MAZURSKY

○-○

Marty, if the man and woman walk away together at the end of the picture, it adds $10,000,000 to the box office.
GEORGE LUCAS to Martin Scorsese

○-○

Don't be too clever for an audience. Make it obvious. Make the subleties obvious also.
BILLY WILDER

Always make the audience suffer as much as possible.
ALFRED HITCHCOCK

My old friend William Wyler used to say, "If you're going to give the audience a shock, just before it, almost reduce them to boredom so that bang, they sit up." He's quite right, of course.
DAVID LEAN

Don't follow trends, start trends.
FRANK CAPRA

It's a matter of suggestion. You kind of tickle the talent.
DAVID LEAN

Remember, no matter how young you are, you are a father figure. Never show yourself to be insecure. RONALD NEAME

An actor entering through the door, you've got nothing. But if he enters through the window, you've got a situation. BILLY WILDER

I am against virtuosity for its own sake. Technique should enrich the action. One doesn't set the camera at a certain angle just because the cameraman happens to be enthusiastic about that spot. The only thing that matters is whether the installation of the camera at a given angle is going to give the scene its maximum impact. The beauty of image and movement, the rhythm and the effects—everything must be subordinated to that purpose. ALFRED HITCHCOCK

It's easy to direct while acting—there's one less person to argue with. ROMAN POLANSKI

o-o-o-o-o-o-o-o-o-o-o-o-o-o-o-o-o-o-o-o-o-o-o-o-o-o-o-o-o-o-o-o

Tell it with pictures. . . . Direct it like you were making a silent. JOHN FORD to Elia Kazan

o-o-o-o-o-o-o-o-o-o-o-o-o-o-o-o-o-o-o-o-o-o-o-o-o-o-o-o-o-o-o-o

Just sit out there and have them go through the moves. When you see something you don't like, change it. JOSHUA LOGAN

Quit now, you'll never make it. If you disregard this advice, you'll be halfway there.

DAVID ZUCKER

The directing of a picture involves coming out of your individual loneliness and taking a controlling part in putting together a small world. A picture is made. You put a frame around it and move on. And one day you die. That is all there is to it. JOHN HUSTON

DRINK

One must always be drunk. Everything is there: it is the essential issue. To avoid that horrible burden of Time grabbing your shoulders and crushing you to the earth, you must get drunk without restraint.   CHARLES BAUDELAIRE

I drink every known alcoholic drink and enjoy 'em all. I learned early in life how to handle alcohol and never had any trouble with it. The rules are simple as mud: first, never drink if you've got any work to do. Never. If I've got a job of work to do at ten o'clock at night I won't take a drink until that time. Secondly, never drink alone. That's the way to become a drunkard. And thirdly, even if you haven't got any work to do, never drink while the sun is shining. Wait until it's dark. By that time you're near enough to bed to recover quickly.

H. L. MENCKEN

First you take a drink, then the drink takes a drink, then the drink takes you.

F. SCOTT FITZGERALD

I think a man ought to get drunk at least twice a year just on principle, so he won't let himself get snotty about it.   RAYMOND CHANDLER

If four or five guys tell you that you're drunk, even though you know you haven't had a thing to drink, the least you can do is to lie down a little while.   JOSEPH SCHENCK

Drink the first. Sip the second slowly. Skip the third.   KNUTE ROCKNE

If you drink, don't drive. Don't even putt.
                                        DEAN MARTIN

You must be careful about giving any drink whatsoever to a bore. A lit-up bore is the worst in the world.   DAVID CECIL

Claret is the liquor for boys; port for men; but he who aspires to be a hero must drink brandy.
                                        SAMUEL JOHNSON

Never refuse wine. It is an odd but universally held opinion that anyone who doesn't drink must be an alcoholic.   P. J. O'ROURKE

A good general rule is to state that the bouquet is better than the taste, and vice versa.

STEPHEN POTTER

The more specific the name, the better the wine.

FRANK SCHOONMAKER

Watch out when the auctioneer calls some nineteenth-century wine "a graceful old lady whose wrinkles are starting to show through layers of makeup." That means the wine is undrinkable, and some fool will spend $500 for it.

ROBERT PARKER

If you drink enough wine, it doesn't matter how bad it is.

ANONYMOUS

It is worse to be drunk with ale or beer than with wine; for the drunkenness endureth longer to the utter ruin of the brain and understanding, by reason that the fumes and vapors of ale or beer that ascend to the head are more gross, and therefore cannot be so soon resolved as those that rise up of wine.

TOBIAS VENNER

They who drink beer will think beer.

WILLIAM WARBURTON

In the summer I drink Guinness, which requires no refrigeration and no cooking—Guinness is a great day-shortener. If you get out of bed first thing and drink a glass, then the day doesn't begin until about twelve-thirty, when you come to again, which is nice. I try to live in a perpetual snooze.   QUENTIN CRISP

There is no bad beer: some kinds are better than others.   GERMAN PROVERB

Brandy and water spoils two good things.
                    CHARLES LAMB

Connoisseurs who like their martinis very dry suggest simply allowing a ray of sunlight to shine through a bottle of Noilly Prat before it hits the gin.   LUIS BUÑUEL

Do not allow children to mix drinks. It is unseemly and they use too much vermouth.
                    FRAN LEBOWITZ

For a bad hangover, take the juice of two quarts of whiskey.   EDDIE CONDON

A good cure for a hangover is to drink black coffee the night before instead of the morning after.   LAURENCE J. PETER

> If you are young and you drink a great deal it will spoil your health, slow your mind, make you fat—in other words, turn you into an adult. Also, if you want to get one of those great red beefy, impressive-looking faces that politicians and corporation presidents have, you had better start drinking early and stick with it.   P. J. O'ROURKE

A man is a fool if he drinks before he reaches fifty, and a fool if he doesn't drink afterward.
             FRANK LLOYD WRIGHT

> The secret to a long life is to stay busy, get plenty of exercise, and don't drink too much. Then again, don't drink too little.
             HERMANN SMITH-JOHANNSON

Water taken in moderation cannot hurt anybody.
             MARK TWAIN

FASHION

A hat should be taken off when you greet a lady and left off for the rest of your life. Nothing looks more stupid than a hat.   P. J. O'ROURKE

Being a well-dressed man is a career, and he who goes in for it has no time for anything else.
HEYWOOD BROUN

A woman who doesn't wear lipstick feels undressed in public. Unless she works on a farm.
MAX FACTOR

Brevity is the soul of lingerie. DOROTHY PARKER

Look for the woman in the dress. If there is no woman, there is no dress.   COCO CHANEL

A woman's dress should be like a barbed-wire fence: serving its purpose without obstructing the view.   SOPHIA LOREN

Violet will be a good color for hair at just about the same time that brunette becomes a good color for flowers. FRAN LEBOWITZ

Mink is for football games . . . please. Out in the fresh air, sit in it, eat hot dogs in it, anything. But not evening, not elegance, I beg of you.
VALENTINA

o-o-o-o-o-o-o-o-o-o-o-o-o-o-o-o-o-o-o-o-o-o-o-o-o-o-o-o-o-o-o-o-o-o

Never wear a suit costing less than two hundred clams.
"LEGS" DIAMOND to Larry Adler

Never wear anything that panics the cat.
P. J. O'ROURKE

When in doubt wear red. BILL BLASS

Brown shoes don't make it. FRANK ZAPPA

Men who wear turtlenecks look like turtles.
DORIS LILLY

Never speak to a man wearing leather trousers.
TOMMY NUTTER

Why not be oneself? That is the whole secret of a successful appearance. If one is a greyhound, why try to look like a Pekingese?   EDITH SITWELL

FATHERLY ADVICE

One of these days in your travels, a guy is going to come up to you and show you a nice, brand-new deck of cards on which the seal is not yet broken, and this guy is going to offer to bet you that he can make the jack of spades jump out of the deck and squirt cider in your ear. But, son, do not bet this man, for as sure as you stand there, you are going to wind up with an earful of cider.

DAMON RUNYON

My dad once gave me a few words of wisdom which I've always tried to live by. He said, "Son, never throw a punch at a redwood."

TOM SELLECK in *Magnum, P.I.*

∞-∞

You have to have a boy. If you don't have a boy, the name dies. And be sure to marry a lady who's young enough to have a baby.

FRANK SINATRA to Frank Sinatra, Jr.

∞-∞

SON: Have you ever smoked opium?

FATHER: Certainly not! Gives you constipation. Dreadful binding effect. Ever see those pictures of the wretched poet Coleridge? Green around the gills. And a stranger to the lavatory. Avoid opium.   JOHN MORTIMER

०-०

Never put whisky into a hot-water bottle crossing borders of dry states or countries. Rubber will spoil taste. Never make love with pants on. Beer on whiskey, very risky. Whisky on beer, never fear. Never eat apples, peaches, pears, etc. while drinking whisky except long French-style dinners, terminating with fruit. Other viands have mollifying effect. Never sleep in moonlight. Known by scientists to induce madness. Should bed stand beside window on clear night draw shades before retiring. Never hold cigar at right angles to fingers. Hayseed. Hold cigar at diagonal. Remove band or not as you prefer. Never wear red necktie. Provide light snorts for ladies if entertaining. Effects of harder stuff on frail sex sometimes disastrous. Bathe in cold water every morning. Painful but exhilarating. Also reduces horniness. Have haircut once a week. Wear dark clothes after 6 P.M. Eat fresh fish for breakfast when available. Avoid kneeling in unheated stone churches. Ecclesiastical dampness causes prematurely gray hair. Fear tastes like a rusty knife and do not let her into your house. Courage tastes of blood. Stand up straight. Admire the world. Relish the love of a gentle woman. Trust in the Lord. JOHN CHEEVER

o-o-o-o-o-o-o-o-o-o-o-o-o-o-o-o-o-o-o-o-o-o-o-o-o-o-o-o-o-o-o-o-o-o-o-o-o-o-o

Have no respect *whatsoever* for authority; forget who said it and instead look at what he starts with, where he ends up, and ask yourself, "Is it reasonable?" RICHARD FEYMAN's father

You want a job where you will never run out of work—be a debt collector.
JOSEPH EPSTEIN's grandfather

Son, you have to guard against speaking more clearly than you think.
HOWARD BAKER's father

Never cry over spilt milk. It could've been whiskey. "PAPPY" MAVERICK, in *Maverick*

My father gave me these hints on speechmaking:
Be sincere . . . be brief . . . be seated.

JAMES ROOSEVELT

Don't change Stevenson just for the fun of rewriting him. You can kill a classic with "improvements." A big, sprawling novel, say *Bleak House,* you have to pare down to a continuity that will hold an audience for ninety or a hundred minutes. But remember, *Jekyll and Hyde* already has a continuity. We don't have to waste time hammering out a story line. What you have to do is visualize it, think of every scene as the camera will see it and not as you—or Stevenson—would describe it in prose.

B. P. SCHULBERG to his son Budd

I remember being upset once and telling my dad I wasn't following through right, and he replied, "Nancy, it doesn't make any difference to a ball what you do after you hit it." NANCY LOPEZ

Be smart, but never show it.

L. B. MAYER to his daughter Edith

When I was made presidential press secretary my father sent me a telegram: "Always tell the truth. If you can't always tell the truth, don't lie."   BILL MOYERS

When I was a small boy, my father told me never to recommend a church or a woman to anyone. And I have found it wise never to recommend a restaurant either. Something always goes wrong with the cheese soufflé.   EDMUND G. LOVE

∘-∘

Having mentioned laughing, I must particularly warn you against it; and I could heartily wish, that you may often be seen to smile; but never be heard to laugh while you live. Frequent and loud laughter is the characteristic of folly and ill manners; it is the manner in which the mob express their silly joy at silly things; and they call it being merry. In my mind, there is nothing so illiberal, and so ill bred, as audible laughter. True wit, or sense, never yet made anybody laugh; they are above it: they please the mind, and give a cheerfulness to the countenance. But it is low buffoonery, or silly accidents, that always excite laughter, and that is what people of sense and breeding should show them selves above. A man's going to sit down, in the supposition that he has a chair behind him, and falling down upon his breech for want of one, sets a whole company a laughing, when all the wit in the world would not do it; a plain proof, in my mind, how low and unbecoming a thing laughter is: not to mention the disagreeable noise that it makes and the shocking distortion of the face that it occasions. Laughter is easily restrained by a very little reflection; but as it is generally connected with the idea of gaiety, people do not enough attend to its absurdity. I am neither of a melancholy nor a cynical disposition, and am as willing and as apt to be pleased as anybody; but I am sure that since I have had the full use of my reason, nobody has ever heard me laugh.

LORD CHESTERFIELD to his son

Son, any white man who has anything to do with a native woman stinks in the eyes of his fellow man. ERROL FLYNN's father

You don't need much [to practice law] except common sense and relatively clean fingernails. JOHN MORTIMER's father

Be wiser than other people if you can, but do not tell them so. LORD CHESTERFIELD to his son

Never fight fair with a stranger, boy. You'll never get out of the jungle that way.

> BEN LOMAN in *Death of a Salesman*
> by Arthur Miller

When [Jack Kennedy] ran for office the first time, he carried a loose-leaf book of quotations around with him. One of them was from his father. "More men die of jealousy than of cancer," it read.

> CHRISTOPHER MATTHEWS

You are a poor girl, and if you don't like to think about it, just ask me. If you don't make up your mind to being that, you become one of those terrible girls that don't know whether they are millionairesses or paupers. You are neither one nor the other.

> F. SCOTT FITZGERALD
> to his daughter Scottie

I have heard a well-built woman compared in her motion to a ship under sail, yet I would advise no wise man to be her owner if her freight be nothing but what she carries between wind and water.

> FRANCIS OSBORNE advising his son not to
> marry a beautiful but poor girl

Never eat a heavily sugared doughnut before you go on TV.

JOHN CHEEVER to his daughter Susan

My pappy told me never to bet my bladder against a brewery or get into an argument with people who buy ink by the barrel.   LANE KIRKLAND

If you can't fight 'em, and they won't let you join 'em, best get out of the country.

"PAPPY" MAVERICK, in *Maverick*

If you run across a restaurant where you often see priests eating with priests, or sporting girls with sporting girls, you may be confident that it is good. Those are two classes of people who like to eat well and get their money's worth.

A. J. LIEBLING

Contrary to popular notion, truck drivers know nothing about good restaurants. If you want a reliable tip, drive into a town, go to the nearest appliance store, and seek out the dishwasher repair man. He spends a lot of time in restaurant kitchens and usually has strong opinions about them.

BRYAN MILLER

Never eat in a restaurant that's over a hundred feet off the ground and won't stand still.

CALVIN TRILLIN

Never trust the food in a restaurant on top of the tallest building in town that spends a lot of time folding napkins.

ANDY ROONEY

Never eat in a restaurant where there's a photo of
the chef with Sammy Davis, Jr. "ALF"

> Never order anything that isn't fried from a wait-
> ress named Mabel; never take the last donut in
> the display case. FLIP SPICELAND

Never eat Chinese food in Oklahoma.
DAVID BRYAN

> When it comes to Chinese food . . . the less known
> about the preparation the better.
> CALVIN TRILLIN

Music with dinner is an insult both to the cook
and the violinist. G. K. CHESTERTON

> At a dinner party one should eat wisely but not
> too well, and talk well but not too wisely.
> W. SOMERSET MAUGHAM

A full belly doth not engender a subtle wit.
GEORGE PETTIE

> Never eat more than you can lift. "MISS PIGGY"

Eat less than you think you want, eat with your intelligence, not your stomach. Never get up from the table with an inward, silent apology for being a pig.   COCO CHANEL

If you would eat well in England, you must eat breakfast three times a day.
                    W. SOMERSET MAUGHAM

Coffee, though a useful medicine, if drunk constantly will at length induce a decay of health, and hectic fever.   JESSE TORREY

Most people just don't know how to make good coffee. In the first place, they boil the water before they put the coffee in. Any fool knows you gotta put the coffee in the cold water and bring 'em both to a boil together. That way you get all the flavor. Worst thing they do, they throw away the old grounds after using them once. What they don't know is they're throwing away the best part. You gotta keep them old grounds an' you add fresh coffee every mornin' an' let 'er boil. Shoot, you don't make a cup, you build a pot.

You don't really get a good pot until you've been usin' it about a week. Then it's coffee.

> DENNIS WEAVER as Chester Goode
> in *Gunsmoke*

Never drink black coffee at lunch; it will keep you awake in the afternoon.   JILLY COOPER

Warm the pot first . . . then put two heaping teaspoonfuls in the pot—no bags—in boiling water, and when it's in, stir it.   LYNN FONTANNE

While it is undeniably true that people love a surprise, it is equally true that they are seldom pleased to suddenly and without warning happen upon a series of prunes in what they took to be a normal loin of pork.   FRAN LEBOWITZ

Pig meat in any form is pretty good in Poland. Everything else except the beer and vodka is horrid. You could use the beef for tennis balls, the bread for hockey pucks, and the mashed potatoes to make library paste. If you swallow any of the gravy, do not induce vomiting. Call a physician immediately.   P. J. O'ROURKE

Don't take a butcher's advice on how to cook meat. If he knew, he'd be a chef.

ANDY ROONEY

Beefsteaks and porter are good belly mortar.

SCOTTISH PROVERB

Nothing helps scenery like ham and eggs.

MARK TWAIN

There are nine ways of poaching eggs, and each of them is worse than the other.   ROBERT LYND

The hymn "Onward Christian Soldiers," sung to the right tune and in a not-too-brisk tempo, makes a very good egg timer. If you put the egg into boiling water and sing all five verses and chorus, the egg will be just right when you come to Amen.

LETTER in the London *Daily Telegraph*

The noise from good toast should reverberate in the head like the thunder of July.   E. V. LUCAS

Bread that must be sliced with an ax is bread that is too nourishing.   FRAN LEBOWITZ

You don't get tired of muffins, but you don't find inspiration in them.   GEORGE BERNARD SHAW

Cheese and salt meat should be sparingly eat.
                          BENJAMIN FRANKLIN

Never commit yourself to a cheese without having first *examined* it.   T. S. ELIOT

You put your left index finger on your eye and your right index finger on the [Camembert]. . . . If they sort of feel the same, the cheese is ready.
                          M. TAITTINGER

Cream . . . is the very head and flower of milk; but it is somewhat of a gross nourishment, and by reason of the unctuosity of it, quickly cloyeth the stomach, relaxeth and weakeneth the retentive faculty thereof, and is easily converted into phlegm, and vaporous fumes.   TOBIAS VENNER

Cucumber should be well sliced, and dressed with pepper and vinegar, and then thrown out, as good for nothing.   SAMUEL JOHNSON

Lettuce is like conversation: it must be fresh and crisp, and so sparkling that you scarcely notice the bitter in it.   CHARLES DUDLEY WARNER

The best peas are the smallest peas and . . . the sleaziest peas are the best peas. WAVERLEY E. ROOT

Artichokes . . . are just plain annoying. . . . After all the trouble you go to, you get about as much actual "food" out of eating an artichoke as you would from licking thirty or forty postage stamps. Have the shrimp cocktail instead. "MISS PIGGY"

Life is too short to stuff a mushroom.
                                        SHIRLEY CONRAN

If you don't know whether a mushroom is edible or not, you cook it all up, and you take a little bit and then you leave it until the next day and watch to see if there are any bad effects. If there aren't any, you eat a little more, and presently you know something.   JOHN CAGE

Never serve oysters during a month that has no paycheck.   P. J. O'ROURKE

Truffles must come to the table in their own stock
... as you break open this jewel sprung from a
poverty-stricken soil, imagine—if you have never
visited it—the desolate kingdom where it rules.

COLETTE

Watermelon—it's a good fruit. You eat, you drink,
you wash your face. ENRICO CARUSO

Don't eat too many almonds; they add weight to
the breasts. COLETTE

Tomatoes and oregano make it Italian; wine and
tarragon make it French. Sour cream makes it
Russian; lemon and cinnamon make it Greek.
Soy sauce makes it Chinese; garlic makes it good.

ALICE MAY BROCK

Shake and shake
The catsup bottle.
None will come,
And then a lot'll.

OGDEN NASH

HOW TO EAT CHOCOLATE CHIP COOKIES
LIKE A CHILD

Half-sit, half-lie on the bed, propped up by a pillow.
Read a book. Place cookies next to you on the sheet so
that crumbs get in the bed. As you eat the cookies,
remove each chocolate chip and place it on your stomach.
When all the cookies are consumed, eat the chips one by
one, allowing two per page. DELIA EPHRON

Mustard's no good without roast beef.
CHICO MARX in *Monkey Business*
(screenplay by S. J. Perelman
and Will B. Johnstone)

Americans can eat garbage, provided you sprin-
kle it liberally with ketchup, mustard, chili sauce,
Tabasco sauce, cayenne pepper, or any other con-
diment which destroys the original flavor of the
dish. HENRY MILLER

The only really good vegetable is Tabasco sauce.
Put Tabasco sauce in everything.
P. J. O'ROURKE

What is sauce for the goose may be sauce for the gander but is not necessarily sauce for the chicken, the duck, the turkey, or the guinea hen.

ALICE B. TOKLAS

Any dish that tastes good with capers in it tastes even better with capers not in it. NORA EPHRON

Don't salt other people's food.

BULGARIAN PROVERB

Serve Coke or RC with meat; 7-Up or Sprite with fish, Dr. Pepper with game . . .

CALVIN TRILLIN

Never eat anything with suction cups. "ALF"

Old people shouldn't eat health foods. They need all the preservatives they can get.

ROBERT ORBEN

Wedding-reception food, whether served at tables or presented at a buffet, should be stuff that's easy to throw up, like spaghetti.

P. J. O'ROURKE

After fish, milk do not wish.

BENJAMIN FRANKLIN

It is almost sure death to eat cucumbers and drink milk at the same meal.   H. L. MENCKEN

Obtain a gross of small white boxes such as are used for a bride's cake. Cut the turkey into small squares, roast, stuff, kill, boil, bake, and allow to skewer. Now we are ready to begin. Fill each box with a quantity of soup stock and pile in a handy place. As the liquid elapses, the prepared turkey is added until the guests arrive. The boxes, delicately tied with white ribbons, are then placed in the handbags of the ladies, or in the men's side pockets.   F. SCOTT FITZGERALD

First prepare the soup of your choice and pour it into a bowl. Then, take the bowl and quickly turn it upside down on the cookie tray. Lift the bowl ever so gently so that the soup retains the shape of the bowl. *Gently* is the key word here. Then, with the knife cut the soup down the middle into halves, then quarters, and *gently* reassemble the soup into a cube. Some of the soup will run off onto the cookie tray. Lift this soup up by the corners and fold slowly into a cylindrical soup staff. Square off the cube by stuffing the cracks with this cylindrical soup staff. Place the packet in your purse or inside coat pocket, and pack off to work.   STEVE MARTIN

> The proper way to cook a cockatoo is to put the bird and an axhead into a billy. Boil them until the axhead is soft. The cockatoo is then ready to eat.   ANONYMOUS

If you have formed the habit of checking on every new diet that comes along, you will find that, mercifully, they all blur together, leaving you with only one definite piece of information: french-fried potatoes are out.   JEAN KERR

> My advice to you is not to inquire why or whither, but just enjoy your ice cream while it's on your plate.   THORTON WILDER

BEN FRANKLIN'S

Wise men don't need advice. Fools don't take it.

> They that will not be counselled, cannot be helped. If you do not hear reason she will rap you on the knuckles.

Ill customs and bad advice are seldom forgotten.

> He that lieth down with dogs, shall rise up with fleas.

If your head is wax, don't walk in the sun.

> A traveller should have a hog's nose, a deer's legs, and an ass's back.

Eat few suppers, and you'll need few medicines.

> You will be careful, if you are wise, how you touch men's religion, or credit, or eyes.

He that hath a trade, hath an estate.

Visit your aunt, but not every day; and call at your brother's, but not every night.

What you would seem to be, be really.

Tart words make no friends: a spoonful of honey will catch more flies than a gallon of vinegar.

Hear reason, or she'll make you feel her.

Make haste slowly.

Neither trust, nor contend, nor lay wagers, nor lend; and you'll have peace to your lives' end.

Eat to live, live not to eat.

Three good meals a day is bad living.

Dine with little, sup with less: do better still: sleep supperless.

To lengthen thy life, lessen thy meals.

An egg today is better than a hen tomorrow.

Eat to please thyself, but dress to please others.

Hold your counsel before dinner; the full belly hates thinking as well as acting.

Take counsel in wine, but resolve afterwards in water.

He that drinks fast, pays slow.

Never praise your cider or your horse.

Observe all men; thyself most.

Search others for their virtues, thyself for thy vices.

Fear to do ill, and you need fear nought else.

Clean your finger before you point at my spots.

When you speak to a man, look on his eyes; when he speaks to thee, look on his mouth.

There's none deceived but he that trusts.

Be civil to all; sociable to many; familiar with few; friend to one; enemy to none.

Drive thy business, or it will drive thee.

Pay what you owe, and what you're worth you'll know.

He that pays for work before it's done, has but a pennyworth for two pence.

If you'd lose a troublesome visitor, lend him money.

Beware of little expenses: a small leak will sink a great ship.

Avoid dishonest gain: no price can recompense the pangs of vice.

If thou injurest conscience, it will have its revenge on thee.

Be not niggardly of what costs thee nothing, as courtesy, counsel, and countenance.

Write injuries in dust, benefits in marble.

Proclaim not all thou knowest, all thou owest, all thou hast, nor all thou can'st.

He that falls in love with himself, will have no rivals.

An ounce of wit that is bought is worth a pound that is taught.

Read much, but not too many books.

Nothing brings more pain than too much pleasure; nothing more bondage than too much liberty, (or libertinism).

Don't throw stones at your neighbors' if your own windows are glass.

When you're an anvil, hold you still; when you're a hammer, strike your fill.

Hear no ill of a friend, nor speak any of an enemy.

If you would keep your secret from an enemy, tell it not to a friend.

To whom thy secret thou dost tell, to him thy freedom thou dost sell.

Love your neighbor; yet don't pull down your hedge.

It is wise not to seek a secret and honest not to reveal it.

Love well, whip well.

He that goes far to marry, will either deceive or be deceived.

Let thy maid servant be faithful, strong, and homely.

Teach your child to hold his tongue; he'll learn fast enough to speak.

If you ride a horse, sit close and tight; if you ride a man, sit easy and light.

Write with the learned, pronounce with the vulgar.

Up, sluggard, and waste not life; in the grave will be sleeping enough.

Wish not so much to live long, as to live well

Work as if you were to live a hundred years, pray as if you were to die tomorrow.

Fear not death; for the sooner we die, the longer we shall be immortal.

If you would not be forgotten, as soon as you are dead and rotten, either write things worth reading, or do things worth the writing.

FRIENDSHIP

To find a friend one must close one eye; to keep him—two.   NORMAN DOUGLAS

It is well, when one is judging a friend, to remember that he is judging you with the same Godlike and superior impartiality.   ARNOLD BENNETT

Never have a friend that's poorer than yourself.
        DOUGLAS JERROLD

Think twice before you speak to a friend in need.
        AMBROSE BIERCE

When one is trying to do something beyond his known powers it is useless to seek the approval of friends. Friends are at their best in moments of defeat.   HENRY MILLER

Few things in life are more embarrassing than the necessity of having to inform an old friend that you have just got engaged to his fiancée.
        W. C. FIELDS

If you want to make a friend, let someone do you
a favor. BENJAMIN FRANKLIN

You can't tell your friend you've been cuckolded;
even if he doesn't laugh at you, he may put the
information to personal use. MONTAIGNE

Don't tell your friends their social faults: they will
cure the fault and never forgive you.
LOGAN PEARSALL SMITH

Don't believe your friends when they ask you to
be honest with them. All they really want is to be
maintained in the good opinion they have of themselves. ALBERT CAMUS

Do not use a hatchet to remove a fly from your
friend's forehead. CHINESE PROVERB

Do not keep on with a mockery of friendship
after the substance is gone—but part, while you
can part friends. Bury the carcass of friendship: it
is not worth embalming. WILLIAM HAZLITT

GAMBLING

Never contend with a man who has nothing to lose.   GRACIAN

It may be that the race is not always to the swift nor the battle to the strong—but that's the way to bet.   DAMON RUNYON

No horse can go as fast as the money you put on it.   EARL WILSON

I know a little bit about handicapping. If the horse has an IV, you want to stay away from it.
                                              PAULA POUNDSTONE

If you are going to bluff, make it a big one.
                        AMARILLO SLIM
                        (THOMAS AUSTIN PRESTON, JR.)

When a man tells me he's going to put all his cards on the table, I always look up his sleeve.
                              LORD LESLIE HORE-BELISHA

Look around the table. If you don't see a sucker, get up, because you're the sucker.   AMARILLO SLIM

When your opponent's sittin' there holdin' all the aces, there's only one thing to do: kick over the table.   DEAN MARTIN

If you want to cure a compulsive gambler, give him the Atlanta Falcons and four points.
PAUL LYNDE

Trust everybody, but cut the cards.
FINLEY PETER DUNNE

One thing that's always available on a golf course is advice. If you play like I do, you think everybody knows something you don't know. If I see a bird fly over, I think he's going to tell me something.
BUDDY HACKETT

The golf swing is like sex: you can't be thinking of the mechanics of the act while you're doing it.
DAVE HILL

Take it easy and lazily, because the golf ball isn't going to run away from you while you're swinging.
SAM SNEAD

That little white ball won't move 'til you hit it, and there's nothing you can do after it's gone.
BABE DIDRIKSON ZAHARIAS

o-o-o-o-o-o-o-o-o-o-o-o-o-o-o-o-o-o-o-o-o-o-o-o-o-o-o-o-o-o-o-o-o-o

Put your ass into the ball, Mr. President.
SAM SNEAD giving a lesson
to Dwight D. Eisenhower

o-o-o-o-o-o-o-o-o-o-o-o-o-o-o-o-o-o-o-o-o-o-o-o-o-o-o-o-o-o-o-o-o-o

Lay off for a few weeks and then quit for good.
SAM SNEAD to a pupil

In case of a thunderstorm, stand in the middle of the fairway and hold up a one-iron. Not even God can hit a one-iron. LEE TREVINO

If you are going to throw a club, it is important to throw it ahead of you, down the fairway, so you don't have to waste energy going back to pick it up. TOMMY BOLT

Never break your putter and driver in the same match or you're dead. TOMMY BOLT

Never do anything stupid. BEN CRENSHAW

Always fade the ball; you can't talk to a hook.
DAVE MARR

There are two things that won't last in this world: dogs chasing cars and pros putting for pars.
LEE TREVINO

Look like a woman, but play like a man.
JAN STEPHENSON

Never bet with a man named "One-Iron."

TOM SHARP

If you break 100, watch your golf. If you break 80, watch your business.   JOEY ADAMS

If the following foursome is pressing you, wave them through and then speed up.

DEANE BEMAN

If a man is notified he has been appointed to serve on the rules committee for a certain tournament he should instantly remember that he must attend an important business meeting in Khartoum.   HERBERT WARREN WIND

Golf . . . combines two favorite American pastimes: taking long walks and hitting things with a stick. Try to tailor your golfing behavior to the low-key, low-pressure spirit of these antecedents. Calm the nerves of fellow players by talking cheerfully to them while they tee off or attempt to one-putt. Help the greenskeeper do his job by making sure that grass roots are well-aerated with divots. Give the caddy a chance to catch up on his aerobic exercises trotting alongside the golf cart with your bag on his shoulder. And don't hit things you aren't supposed to. An important aspect of golf is knowing what to hit.   P. J. O'ROURKE

Being left-handed is a big advantage: no one knows enough about your swing to mess you up with advice.   BOB CHARLES

HAPPINESS

All you need for happiness is a good gun, a good horse, and a good wife.   DANIEL BOONE

All happiness depends on a leisurely breakfast.
JOHN GUNTHER

Happiness seems to require a modicum of external prosperity.   ARISTOTLE

To fall in love with yourself is the first secret of happiness. I did so at the age of four-and-a-half. Then if you're not a good mixer you can always fall back on your own company.
ROBERT MORLEY

Pleasure is the only thing to live for. Nothing ages like happiness.   OSCAR WILDE

The secret of happiness is to find a congenial monotony.   V. S. PRITCHETT

The only way to avoid being miserable is not to have enough leisure to wonder whether you are happy or not.   GEORGE BERNARD SHAW

If you get gloomy, just take an hour off and sit and think how much better this world is than hell. Of course, it won't cheer you up if you expect to go there.   DON MARQUIS

When you jump for joy, beware that no one moves the ground from beneath your feet.
                                            STANISLAW LEC

We must select the illusion which appeals to our temperament and embrace it with passion, if we want to be happy.   CYRIL CONNOLLY

A solved problem creates two new problems, and the best prescription for happy living is not to solve any more problems than you have to.
                                            RUSSELL BAKER

If only we'd stop trying to be happy we'd have a pretty good time.   EDITH WHARTON

HEALTH

The only way to keep your health is to eat what you don't want, drink what you don't like, and do what you'd rather not.　　MARK TWAIN

> Early to rise and early to bed makes a male healthy and wealthy and dead.　JAMES THURBER

Eat only when you're hungry. Drink only when you're thirsty. Sleep only when you're tired. Screw only when you're horny.　　AL NEUHARTH

> The trouble with always trying to preserve the health of the body is that it is so difficult to do without destroying the health of the mind.
> 　　G. K. CHESTERTON

It is better to lose health like a spendthrift than to waste it like a miser, better to live and be done with it, than to die daily in the sick room.
　　ROBERT LOUIS STEVENSON

> Beware of the young doctor and the old barber.
> 　　BENJAMIN FRANKLIN

○-○

The actress Billy Burke was dining in a restaurant where at the next table a man was obviously suffering from a bad cold. "I can see you're very uncomfortable," she volunteered. "So I'll tell you what to do for it: drink lots of orange juice and take lots of aspirin. When you go to bed, cover yourself with as many blankets as you can find. Sweat the cold out. Believe me, I know what I'm talking about. I am Billie Burke of Hollywood." The man smiled and introduced himself in return: "Thank you. I am Dr. Mayo of the Mayo Clinic."

○-○

Keep away from physicians. It is all probing and guessing and pretending with them. They leave it to Nature to cure in her own time, but they take the credit. As well as very fat fees.

ANTHONY BURGESS

This warning from the New York City Department of Health Fraud: Be suspicious of any doctor who tries to take your temperature with his finger.

DAVID LETTERMAN

Never go to a doctor whose office plants have died.

ERMA BOMBECK

It is a good idea to "shop around" before you settle on a doctor. Ask about the condition of his Mercedes. Ask about the competence of his mechanic. Don't be shy! After all you're paying for it.

DAVE BARRY

One should only see a psychiatrist out of boredom.

MURIEL SPARK

Anybody who goes to see a psychiatrist ought to have his head examined.

SAMUEL GOLDWYN

o-o-o-o-o-o-o-o-o-o-o-o-o-o-o-o-o-o-o-o-o-o-o-o-o-o-o-o-o-o-o-o

The British medical journal the *Lancet* advises against social kissing because it spreads multitudes of noisome germs. At a wedding, for example, kissing the bride exposes you to germs deposited on her cheek by the guests before you. But if you must buss the bride, *Lancet* advises: "Either make sure you are near the front of the queue or, before applying the lips, wipe the bride's cheeks gently with a diluted solution of hypochlorite (an antiseptic)."

o-o-o-o-o-o-o-o-o-o-o-o-o-o-o-o-o-o-o-o-o-o-o-o-o-o-o-o-o-o-o-o

A high-fiber breakfast is very important. Always eat your cereal before it shrinks.

MARK RUSSELL

If you want to clear your system out, sit on a piece of cheese and swallow a mouse.

JOHNNY CARSON

Sunburn is very becoming—but only when it is even—one must be careful not to look like a mixed grill. NOEL COWARD

○-○

Robert Benchley gave this unsolicited advice to an acquaintance who had made several unsuccessful suicide attempts: "You want to go easy on the suicide stuff—first thing you know, you'll ruin your health."

○-○

Always do one thing less than you think you can do. BERNARD BARUCH

Never touch your eye but with your elbow.

ENGLISH PROVERB

Wash your hands often, your feet seldom, and your head never. JOHN RAY

If you go long enough without a bath, even the fleas will let you alone. ERNIE PYLE

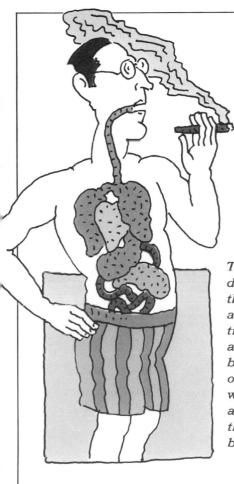

Tobacco drieth the brain, dimmeth the sight, vitiateth the smell, hurteth the stomach, destroyeth the concoction, disturbeth the humors and spirits, corrupteth the breath, induceth a trembling of the limbs, exiccateth the windpipe, lungs and liver, annoyeth the milt, scorcheth the heart, and causeth the blood to be adjusted.

TOBIAS VENNER

Supreme Court Justice William J. Brennan felt faint while working at his desk and was rushed to a nearby hospital, where he was diagnosed with pneumonia. He was admitted to the hospital, was found to be suffering from a gallbladder condition as well, and doctors removed it. Soon thereafter former Chief Justice Burger was admitted to another hospital with pneumonia. Justice Brennan called him with the advice: "Warren, you'd better get out of there quickly. If they think you have pneumonia, they'll take your gallbladder out."

A cure for bags under the eyes: sleep upside down and the bags will often work through to a less noticeable part of the body.   MARY DUNN

The best cure for hypochondria is to forget about your body and get interested in someone else's.
GOODMAN ACE

I have a perfect cure for a sore throat: cut it.
ALFRED HITCHCOCK

INVESTMENT

Buy on the cannons, sell on the trumpets.
FRENCH ADAGE

Buy on the rumor, sell on the news.
WALL STREET ADAGE

Buy when there's blood in the streets.
BARON GUY DE ROTHSCHILD

Never buy at the bottom, and always sell too soon.
JESSE L. LIVERMORE

Don't try to buy at the bottom and sell at the top. This can't be done—except by liars.
BERNARD BARUCH

Buy old masters. They fetch a much better price than old mistresses.
LORD BEAVERBROOK

Invest in inflation. It's the only thing going up.
WILL ROGERS

Never invest in anything that eats or needs painting.
BILLY ROSE

Any policy leading to portfolio turnover is like one leading to war or litigation: it's self-destructive, enriches the wrong people, and cancels out in the end.
JOHN TRAIN

There is nothing so disastrous as a rational investment policy in an irrational world.
JOHN MAYNARD KEYNES

Bulls can make money and bears can make money, but hogs just get slaughtered.
WALL STREET ADAGE

Stay in love with a security until the security gets overvalued, then let somebody else fall in love with it.
ROY NEUBERGER

Don't gamble. Take all your savings and buy some good stock and hold it 'til it goes up, then sell it. If it don't go up, don't buy it.
WILL ROGERS

Put all your eggs in one basket, and watch the basket.   MARK TWAIN

The safest way to double your money is to fold it over once and put it in your pocket.
                                        KIN HUBBARD

There are two times in a man's life when he should not speculate: when he can't afford it, and when he can.   MARK TWAIN

JOURNALISM

Never lose your sense of the superficial.
>   LORD NORTHCLIFFE

> The only qualities for real success in journalism
> are ratlike cunning, a plausible manner, and a
> little literary ability. The capacity to steal other
> people's ideas and phrases . . . is also invaluable.
>   NICHOLAS TOMALIN

Like Latin, journalese is primarily a written language, prized for its incantory powers, and is best learned early while the mind is still supple. Every cub reporter, for instance, knows that fires rage out of control, minor mischief is perpetrated by vandals (never Visigoths, Franks, or one Vandal working alone), and key labor accords are hammered out by weary negotiators in marathon, round-the-clock bargaining sessions, thus narrowly averting threatened walkouts. The discipline required for a winter storm report is awesome. The first reference to seasonal precipitation is "snow," followed by "the white stuff," then either "it" or "the flakes," but not both. The word *snow* may be used once again toward the end of the report, directly after discussion of ice-slicked roads and grim highway toll.   JOHN LEO

> Do your homework and keep good files. Know the background and biases of your sources.
>
> JANE BRODY

Never . . . know a public man well enough that he inhibits you from writing about him frankly and fully while he's living his public life.

ALISTAIR COOKE

> The only way a reporter should look at a politician is down.   VIC GOLD

Never sound excited. Imagine yourself at a dinner table back in the United States with the local editor, a banker, and a professor talking over coffee. You try to tell what it was like, while the maid's boyfriend, a truck driver, listens from the kitchen. Try to be understood by the truck driver while not insulting the professor's intelligence.

EDWARD R. MURROW
to a young war correspondent

Learn to write. Never mind the damn statistics. If you like statistics become a CPA.
JIM MURRAY to young sportswriters

Read. And think. But as little as possible about sports. THOMAS BOSWELL to sportswriters

Remember, you only have that space because some advertiser wouldn't buy it.
HERB CAEN to columnists

Learn to type and take some kind of shorthand notes. Read everything to do with history, biography, English, art, music. Absorb culture. Study human nature. Develop and maintain your sense of humor and irony. And don't be too ridiculous because your name over the column isn't really so important. LIZ SMITH

Be less curious about people and more curious about ideas.
MARIE CURIE's standard advice to reporters seeking interviews.

The plain truth is that the reporter's trade is for young men. Your feet, which do the legwork, are nine times more important than your head, which fits the facts into a coherent pattern.

JOSEPH W. ALSOP, JR.

o-o-o-o-o-o-o-o-o-o-o-o-o-o-o-o-o-o-o-o-o-o-o-o-o-o-o-o-o-o-o-o-o-o-o-o-o-o

GO TO JOURNALISM SCHOOL

The history of journalism is about as exciting as the history of men's hats. There's absolutely no reason to study it in college except for the vast network of journalism schools which have to put something on the menu that no one else has. So instead of getting a *real* education, go to journalism school and learn how to write like everybody else.

PRINT VS. BROADCAST

If you don't understand journalism but you can read a sentence—particularly an underlined part of it—you probably belong in broadcast journalism. Make sure you have several hair dryers. If you have a scar anywhere on your face, you'll have to go into print journalism.

COVERING OUR NATION'S CAPITAL

In Washington, it's important to report exactly what every other reporter is reporting that day. It's tacky to be writing about the national debt or the unannounced invasion of a small country when everyone else is writing about Gary Hart's love life. It's like leaving The Tour and it's very dangerous; you're thought to be eccentric if you do any work apart from the pack. So wait until the other guy is finished and then read *his* copy before filing your own.

And remember that the White House Press Corps is culled from people who are biologically unable to break a news story. Your job at the White House is to serve as a conduit for Presidential pap, and if you attempt to go beyond it you'll be frozen out and you won't get your dose of pap the next day. The only reporters who are assigned to the White House in the first place are those who have already retired or who are unable to report because of one deformity or another. It's the same as being given the San Francisco bureau: it means that you're at the end of the line.

YOUR CREDO

Reality is just something that a good journalist hangs his opinions on, so ignore the external world as much as possible and report your own views. Everybody knows that journalists are smarter than everybody else, and your job is to demonstrate that. JOHN LEO

When the law is on your side, argue the law.
When the facts are on your side, argue the facts.
When neither the facts nor the law are on your
side, make an ad hominem attack.   OLD ADAGE

When the law is on your side, argue the law.
When the facts are on your side, argue the facts.
When neither the facts nor the law are on your
side, holler.   SENATOR ALBERT GORE, JR.

First rule of murder: never ask the customer if
they did it—in case they tell you.
HORACE RUMPOLE (JOHN MORTIMER)

Never ask a question of a witness if you don't
already know the answer.   OLD ADAGE

If they ever give you a brief . . . attack the medical evidence. Remember, the jury's full of rheu-
matism and arthritis and shocking gastric troubles.
They love to see a medical man put through it.
JOHN MORTIMER

Be prepared, be sharp, be careful, and use the King's English well. And you can forget all the [other rules] unless you remember one more: get paid.   ROBERT N. C. NIX

Quote Learned but follow Gus.
          ANONYMOUS (Learned Hand and his less eloquent but more pragmatic cousin, Augustus, both sat on the U.S. Court of Appeals)

Don't shake hands [in the courthouse] with colleagues; the customers think you're making deals.
          HORACE RUMPOLE (JOHN MORTIMER)

Treat the bailiff with respect. He has a gun.
                              MALCOLM LEWIS

Life is like a sewer—you get out of it what you
put into it.   TOM LEHRER

There is more to life than increasing its speed.
                                              GANDHI

Always stay in your own movie.   KEN KESEY

Our life is frittered away by detail . . . simplify,
simplify.   THOREAU

If you step on people in this life, you're going to
come back as a cockroach.   WILLIE DAVIS

Don't be sharp or flat; just be natural.
                                      WILLIE STARGELL

Own only what you can always carry with you;
know languages, know countries, know people.
Let your memory be your travel bag.
                          ALEXANDER SOLZHENITSYN

Live fast, die young, and leave a good-looking corpse.　　JOHN DEREK in *Knock on Any Door*
(screenplay by Willard Motley)

Forget living well. The best revenge is revenge.
WILLIAM HAMILTON

I advise you to go on living solely to enrage those who are paying your annuities. It is the only pleasure I have left.　　VOLTAIRE

Learn young about hard work and manners—and you'll be through the whole dirty mess and nicely dead again before you know it.
F. SCOTT FITZGERALD

All men should strive to learn before they die what they are running from, and to, and why.
JAMES THURBER

Life is like a dogsled team. If you ain't the lead dog, the scenery never changes.
LEWIS GRIZZARD

Life is too short to balance a checkbook.
HOWARD OGDEN

If you're small, you better be a winner.
                                    BILLIE JEAN KING

Life can only be understood backward, but it must be lived forward.   KIERKEGAARD

The first thing in life is to assume a pose. What the second one is, no one has yet discovered.
                                    OSCAR WILDE

All sorrows can be borne if you tell a story about them.   KAREN BLIXEN

Suffering is overrated. It doesn't teach you anything.   BILL VEECK

Do something for the joy of doing it and pray you won't be punished.   SAMMY CAHN

Live all you can; it's a mistake not to. It doesn't so much matter what you do in particular, so long as you have your life. If you haven't had that, what have you had?   HENRY JAMES

There are only two ways to live your life. One is as though nothing is a miracle. The other is as though everything is a miracle.

ALBERT EINSTEIN

There are two things that one must get used to or one will find life unendurable: the damages of time and injustices of men.   NICOLAS CHAMFORT

You can and you can't
You shall and you shan't;
You will and you won't
You'll be damned if you do,
And you'll be damned if you don't.

LORENZO DOW

Life is not so bad if you have plenty of luck, a good physique, and not too much imagination.

CHRISTOPHER ISHERWOOD

The contemplative life is often miserable. One must act more, think less, and not watch oneself live.   NICOLAS CHAMFORT

What good are vitamins? Eat four lobsters, eat a pound of caviar—live! If you are in love with a beautiful blonde with an empty face and no brain at all, don't be afraid, marry her—live!   ARTUR RUBINSTEIN

○-○

Many years ago a very wise man named Bernard Baruch took me aside and put his arm around my shoulder. "Harpo my boy," he said, "I'm going to give you three pieces of advice, three things you should always remember." My heart jumped and I glowed with expectation. I was going to hear the magic password to a rich, full life from the master himself. "Yes sir?" I said. And he told me the three things. I regret that I've forgotten what they were.   HARPO MARX

○-○

It is better to wear out than to rust out.
                              RICHARD CUMBERLAND

            Eat cereal for breakfast and write good prose.
                                    RAYMOND CARVER

Hope for the best. Expect the worst.
Life is a play. We're unrehearsed.   MEL BROOKS

            If you don't think too good, don't think too much.
                                          TED WILLIAMS

The one serious conviction that a man should
have is that nothing should be taken too seriously.
                              NICHOLAS MURRAY BUTLER

The secret of life is to appreciate the pleasure of being terribly deceived.   OSCAR WILDE

Life moves pretty fast; you don't stop and look around every once in a while, you could miss it.
MATTHEW BRODERICK in *Ferris Bueller's Day Off* (screenplay by John Hughes)

When you talk to the half-wise, twaddle; when you talk to the ignorant, brag; when you talk to the sagacious, look very humble and ask their opinion.   EDWARD BULWER-LYTTON

Do not try to live forever. You will not succeed.
GEORGE BERNARD SHAW

Life is a shit sandwich. But if you've got enough bread, you don't taste the shit.
JONATHAN WINTERS

One should try everything once, except incest and folk dancing.   ARNOLD BAX

Life is too short to do anything for oneself that one can pay others to do for one.
W. SOMERSET MAUGHAM

The great secret of life . . . [is] not to open your letters for a fortnight. At the expiration of that period you will find that nearly all of them have answered themselves.   ARTHUR BINSTEAD

You can't learn too soon that the most useful thing about a principle is that it can always be sacrificed to expediency.

W. SOMERSET MAUGHAM

There are two things to aim at in life: first, to get what you want; and after that to enjoy it. Only the wisest of mankind achieve the second.

LOGAN PEARSALL SMITH

Try to arrange your life in such a way that you can afford to be disinterested. It is the most expensive of all luxuries, and the one best worth having.   WILLIAM INGE

Gullibility is the key to all adventures. The greenhorn is the ultimate victor in everything; it is he that gets the most out of life.

G. K. CHESTERTON

The more crap you believe, the better off you are. CHARLES BUKOWSKI

Follow your bliss. JOSEPH CAMPBELL

Take care to sell your horse before he dies. The art of life is passing losses on. ROBERT FROST

Don't be afraid your life will end; be afraid that it will never begin. GRACE HANSEN

Do not fear death so much, but rather the inadequate life. BERTOLT BRECHT

The idea is to die young as late as possible. ASHLEY MONTAGU

Be honest with yourself until the end of your life. Then listen to the slow movement of the Schubert Quintet and kick the bucket. NATHAN MILSTEIN

I recommend having no relationships except those easily borne and disposed of; I recommend limiting one's involvement in other people's lives to a pleasantly scant minimum.   QUENTIN CRISP

> It's possible to love a human being if you don't know them too well.   CHARLES BUKOWSKI

○-○

I used to call [Count Basie] one of my lawyers. He would give me such beautiful advice. And he would phrase that advice into these little sayings. One saying of Count Basie's that I'll always remember pertains to when my husband and I broke up. Basie said, It's just like a toothache. It hurts now, but if you take that tooth out, you'll miss it but you'll feel better.   ELLA FITZGERALD

○-○

When a couple decides to divorce, they should inform both sets of parents before having a party and telling all their friends. This is not only courteous but practical. Parents may be very willing

to pitch in with comments, criticism, and malicious gossip of their own to help the divorce along.
                                        P. J. O'ROURKE

One should always be wary of someone who promises that their love will last longer than a weekend.
                                        QUENTIN CRISP

It is very difficult to maintain a relationship based solely on mistrust.
        PIERCE BROSNAN in *Remington Steele*

o-o-o-o-o-o-o-o-o-o-o-o-o-o-o-o-o-o-o-o-o-o-o-o-o-o-o-o-o-o-o-o-o

On a television show on which celebrity panelists attempted to solve marital problems, Zsa Zsa Gabor was asked, "Mis Gabor, although my fiancé has given me diamonds, a mink coat, an expensive automobile, and a stove, I'm going to break up with him. What should I do?" Without hesitating, Zsa Zsa replied, "Give back the stove."

o-o-o-o-o-o-o-o-o-o-o-o-o-o-o-o-o-o-o-o-o-o-o-o-o-o-o-o-o-o-o-o-o

LYING

If you tell a lie, always rehearse it. If it don't sound good to you, it won't sound good to anybody.　　　　　　　　　　　SATCHEL PAIGE

Look wise, say nothing, and grunt: speech was given to conceal thought.　　WILLIAM OSTLER

Frank and explicit—that is the right line to take when you wish to conceal your own mind and confuse the minds of others.　BENJAMIN DISRAELI

One should be just as careful about lying as about telling the truth.　　　　　LYTTON STRACHEY

Don't lie if you don't have to.　　　LEO SZILARD

If one cannot invent a really convincing lie, it is often better to stick to the truth.
　　　　　　　　　　　ANGELA THIRKELL

It takes a wise man to handle a lie; a fool had better remain honest.　　NORMAN DOUGLAS

If you want to be thought a liar, always tell the truth. LOGAN PEARSALL SMITH

If you do not wish to be lied to, do not ask questions. If there were no questions, there would be no lies. B. TRAVEN

Never lie when the truth is more profitable. STANISLAW LEC

Always tell the truth—it's the easiest thing to remember. DAVID MAMET

If at first you don't succeed, lie, lie again. LAURENCE J. PETER

You don't tell deliberate lies, but sometimes you have to be evasive. MARGARET THATCHER

No man has a good enough memory to be a successful liar. ABRAHAM LINCOLN

Actions lie louder than words. CAROLYN WELLS

A little sincerity is a dangerous thing, and a great deal of it is absolutely fatal. OSCAR WILDE

It is dangerous to be sincere unless you are also
stupid.   GEORGE BERNARD SHAW

There is one way to find out if a man is honest—
ask him. If he says yes, you know he is crooked.
                                 GROUCHO MARX

It is hard to believe that a man is telling the truth
when you know that you would lie if you were in
his place.   H. L. MENCKEN

If one is to be called a liar, one may as well make
an effort to deserve the name.   A. A. MILNE

The surest way to convey misinformation is to
tell the strict truth.   MARK TWAIN

Some people will believe anything if you whisper
it to them.   LOUIS NIZER

Honesty is a good thing, but it is not profitable to
its possessor unless it is kept under control.
                                 DON MARQUIS

It is better to be quotable than to be honest.
                                 TOM STOPPARD

MARRIAGE

By all means marry; if you get a good wife, you'll be happy. If you get a bad one, you'll become a philosopher. SOCRATES

Get married, but never to a man who is home all day. GEORGE BERNARD SHAW

If you want to sacrifice the admiration of many men for the criticism of one, go ahead, get married. KATHARINE HEPBURN

People marry for a variety of reasons, and with varying results; but to marry for love is to invite inevitable tragedy. JAMES BRANCH CABELL

If you are afraid of loneliness, do not marry. CHEKHOV

A man who desires to get married should know everything or nothing. GEORGE BERNARD SHAW

Only choose in marriage a woman whom you would choose as a friend if she were a man. JOSEPH JOUBERT

Every woman should marry—and no man.
BENJAMIN DISRAELI

It is most unwise for people in love to marry.
GEORGE BERNARD SHAW

Never marry a beautiful woman.   H. G. WELLS

You can't be happy with a woman who pronounces
both *d*'s in Wednesday.   PETER DE VRIES

A man must marry only a very pretty woman in
case he should ever want some other man to take
her off his hands.   SACHA GUITRY

You'll need [pornography]. Lots of it. The dirty,
filthy, degrading kind. But keep it *well hidden*!
Don't discount secret wall panels, trick drawers,
holes in the yard, etc., especially if you have
teenage boys or a Baptist wife with a houseclean-
ing obsession. Also keep in mind that you could
die at any moment, and nothing puts a crimp in a
funeral worse than having the bereaved family
wonder what kind of sick, perverted beast you
were under that kind and genteel exterior.
JOHN HUGHES

The husband who wants a happy marriage should learn to keep his mouth shut and his checkbook open.

GROUCHO MARX

No man should marry before he has studied anatomy and dissected the body of a woman.

BALZAC

Keep your eyes wide open before marriage, half shut afterwards. BENJAMIN FRANKLIN

Never get married in the morning—you never know who you might meet that night.

PAUL HORNUNG

Never get married while you're going to college; it's hard to get a start if a prospective employer finds you've already made one mistake.

KIN HUBBARD

Marry an orphan: you'll never have to spend boring holidays with the in-laws (at most an occasional visit to the cemetery). GEORGE CARLIN

◇-◇

Oscar Levant to Harpo Marx upon meeting Harpo's fiancée: "Harpo, she's a lovely person. She deserves a good husband. Marry her before she finds one."

◇-◇

Marry her, Charlie. Just because she's a thief and a hitter doesn't mean she isn't a good woman in all the other departments.

> ANJELICA HUSTON to Jack Nicholson in *Prizzi's Honor* (screenplay by Richard Condon and Janet Roach)

Once you are married there is nothing left for you, not even suicide, but to be good.

> ROBERT LOUIS STEVENSON

Never go to bed mad. Stay up and fight.

> PHYLLIS DILLER

Separate bedrooms and separate bathrooms.

> BETTE DAVIS

I think a man can have two, maybe three affairs while he is married. But three is the absolute maximum. After that, you are cheating.

> YVES MONTAND

Long engagements give people the opportunity of finding out each other's character before marriage, which is never advisable.   OSCAR WILDE

A Code of Honor: Never approach a friend's girlfriend or wife with mischief as your goal. There are just too many women in the world to justify that sort of dishonorable behavior. Unless she's *really* attractive.   BRUCE JAY FRIEDMAN

Intellectuals should never marry; they won't enjoy it; and besides, they should not reproduce themselves.   DON HEROLD

A girl must marry for love, and keep on marrying until she finds it.   ZSA ZSA GABOR

∘⟡∘

We'll lead an ideal life if you'll just avoid doing one thing: don't think.   RONALD REAGAN to
then-wife Jane Wyman

∘⟡∘

Bigamy is one way of avoiding the painful publicity of divorce and the expense of alimony.   OLIVER HERFORD

It is most dangerous nowadays for a husband to pay any attention to his wife in public. It always makes people think that he beats her when they are alone. OSCAR WILDE

Never marry a girl named "Marie" who used to be known as "Murray." JOHNNY CARSON

A good man doesn't just happen. They have to be created by us women. A guy is a lump like a doughnut. So, first you gotta get rid of all the stuff his mom did to him. And then you gotta get rid of all that macho crap that they pick up from beer commercials. And then there's my personal favorite, the male ego.   ROSEANNE BARR

If you talk about yourself, he'll think you're boring. If you talk about others, he'll think you're a gossip. If you talk about him, he'll think you're a brilliant conversationalist.   LINDA SUNSHINE

Never refer to any part of his body below his waist as "cute" or "little"; never expect *him* to do anything about birth control; never ask if he changes his sheets seasonally; never request that *he* sleep on the wet spot.   C. E. CRIMMINS

Beware of men who cry. It's true that men who cry are sensitive to and in touch with feelings, but the only feelings they tend to be sensitive to and in touch with are their own.   NORA EPHRON

An absence, the decline of a dinner invitation, an unintentional coldness, can accomplish more than all the cosmetics and beautiful dresses in the world.
MARCEL PROUST

If you're willing to travel, or just super-desperate, the best place in the world to meet unattached men is on the Alaska pipeline. I'm told that the trek through the frozen tundra is well worth the effect for any woman who wants to know what it feels like to be Victoria Principal.
LINDA SUNSHINE

If you never want to see a man again, say, "I love you, I want to marry you. I want to have children . . ."—they leave skid marks.
RITA RUDNER

Don't accept rides from strange men—and remember that all men are as strange as hell.
ROBIN MORGAN

Money is like manure. If you spread it around it does a lot of good, but if you pile it up in one place it stinks like hell.   CLINT MURCHISON

Get money first; virtue comes afterward.

HORACE

Money isn't everything as long as you have enough.   MALCOLM FORBES

Seek wealth, it's good.   IVAN BOESKY

Leo, he who hesitates is poor.
ZERO MOSTEL in *The Producers*
(screenplay by Mel Brooks)

Don't wait for pie in the sky when you die! Get yours now, with ice cream on top!
REVEREND IKE
(FREDERICK J. EIKERENKOETTER II)

Where large sums of money are concerned, it is advisable to trust nobody.   AGATHA CHRISTIE

The thing to do is to make so much money that you don't have to work after the age of twenty-seven. In case this is impracticable, stop work at the earliest possible moment, even if it is a quarter past eleven in the morning of the day when you find you have enough money.

ROBERT BENCHLEY

Those who set out to serve both God and Mammon soon discover there is no God.

LOGAN PEARSALL SMITH

I've been rich and I've been poor, and believe me, rich is better.   JOE E. LEWIS

Money is better than poverty, if only for financial reasons.   WOODY ALLEN

Never steal more than you actually need, for the possession of surplus money leads to extravagance, foppish attire, frivolous thought.

DALTON TRUMBO

Anybody can make a fortune. It takes genius to hold on to one.   JAY GOULD

When a fellow says, "It ain't the money, but the principle of the thing," it's the money.

KIN HUBBARD

Always live within your income, even if you have to borrow money to do so. JOSH BILLINGS

Anyone who lives within his means suffers from a lack of imagination. LIONEL STANDER

Annual income twenty pounds, annual expenditure nineteen nineteen six, result happiness. Annual income twenty pounds, annual expenditure twenty pounds ought and six, result misery.

CHARLES DICKENS

Never run into debt, not if you can find anything else to run into. JOSH BILLINGS

Who tells a lie to save his credit wipes his nose on his sleeve to save his napkin. JAMES HOWELL

Saving is a very fine thing. Especially when your parents have done it for you.

WINSTON CHURCHILL

Simple rules for saving money: to save half, when you are fired by an eager impulse to contribute to a charity, wait and count forty. To save three-quarters, count sixty. To save it all, count sixty-five. MARK TWAIN

It is not economical to go to bed early to save the candles if the result is twins. CHINESE PROVERB

If you would know the value of money, go and try to borrow some. BENJAMIN FRANKLIN

To borrow money, big money, you have to wear your hair in a certain way, walk in a certain way, and have about you an air of solemnity and majesty—something like the atmosphere of a Gothic cathedral. STEPHEN LEACOCK

The mortgage market changes virtually from day to day, so you can wait a few weeks and, if you haven't committed suicide in the meantime, try again, even with the same lenders.
WILLIAM G. CONNOLLY

Never give your money away to your children in your lifetime. Always keep control. If you don't, if you listen to the lawyers and the accountants, you'll find yourself being led up the steps of the nursing home.   JOHN D. SPOONER

If you want him to mourn, you had best leave him nothing.   MARTIAL

If a man dies and leaves his estate in an uncertain condition, the lawyers become his heirs.

ED HOWE

He who gives while he lives
Also knows where it goes.   PERCY ROSS

When you have told anyone you have left him a legacy, the only decent thing to do is die at once.

SAMUEL BUTLER

It's better to give than to lend, and it costs about the same.   PHILIP GIBBS

You can't put your VISA bill on your American Express card.   P. J. O'ROURKE

Attend no auctions if thou hast no money.

THE TALMUD

The advantage of keeping family accounts is clear. If you do not keep them, you are uneasily aware of the fact that you are spending more than you are earning. If you do keep them, you *know* it.

ROBERT BENCHLEY

Never ask of money spent
Where the spender thinks it went.
Nobody was ever meant
To remember or invent
What he did with every cent.

ROBERT FROST

There are several ways to apportion the family income, all of them unsatisfactory.

ROBERT BENCHLEY

The best way to keep money in perspective is to have some.

LOUIS RUKEYSER

It is better to have a permanent income than to be fascinating.

OSCAR WILDE

A lot of people will urge you to put some money in a bank, and in fact—within reason—this is very good advice. But don't go overboard. Remember, what you are doing is giving your money to someone else to hold on to, and I think that it is worth keeping in mind that the businessmen who run banks are so worried about holding on to things that they put little chains on all their pens.

"MISS PIGGY"

One rule which woe betides the banker who fails to heed it . . . Never lend any money to anybody unless they don't need it. OGDEN NASH

Is this the sort of advice you're looking for?—Make money. Make it, if you can, fair and square. If not, make it anyway. HORACE

Always try to rub up against money, for if you rub up against money long enough, some of it may rub off on you. DAMON RUNYON

The great rule is not to talk about money with people who have much more or much less than you. KATHARINE WHITEHORN

Nobody works as hard for his money as the man
who marries it.   KIN HUBBARD

There is only one thing for a man to do who is
married to a woman who enjoys spending money,
and that is to enjoy earning it.   ED HOWE

Money can't buy friends, but you can get a better
class of enemy.   SPIKE MILLIGAN

Money won't buy happiness, but it will pay the
salaries of a large research staff to study the
problem.   BILL VAUGHAN

The man who tips a shilling every time he stops
for petrol is giving away annually the cost of
lubricating his car.   J. PAUL GETTY

People will swim through shit if you put a few
bob in it.   PETER SELLERS

To be clever enough to get a great deal of money,
one must be stupid enough to want it.
                        GEORGE BERNARD SHAW

It's no trick to make a lot of money, if all you
want to do is make a lot of money.
>EVERETT SLOANE in *Citizen Kane*
>(screenplay by Herman Mankiewicz and
>Orson Welles)

>If you've got it, flaunt it!
>>ZERO MOSTEL in *The Producers*
>>(screenplay by Mel Brooks)

No man will take counsel, but every man will
take money; therefore, money is better than counsel.   JONATHAN SWIFT

My mother told me, "Elwood,"—she always called me "Elwood"—"in this world you must be oh so smart or oh so pleasant. Well, for years I was smart. I recommend pleasant."

> JAMES STEWART as Elwood P. Dowd in *Harvey* (screenplay by Mary Chase and Oscar Brodney)

My mother, Southern to the bone, once told me, "All Southern literature can be summed up in these words: 'On the night the hogs ate Willie, Mama died when she heard what Daddy did to sister.' "
PAT CONROY

Never take shit from nobody.

> JENNY DOWNEY to her son, Billy Martin

You are a member of the British royal family. We are *never* tired, and we all *love* hospitals.

> QUEEN MARY to her daughter, Queen Elizabeth II

Stay away from Russia. If you go to Moscow you'll get yourself arrested and end up in the salt mines.　　　NICHOLAS DANILOFF's grandmother to her grandson.

Advice to expectant mothers: you must remember that when you are pregnant, you are eating for two. But you must also remember that the other one of you is about the size of a golf ball, so let's not go overboard with it. I mean, a lot of pregnant women eat as though the other person they're eating for is Orson Welles.　DAVE BARRY

Advice to young mothers: if you are truly young, then you should wait a couple of decades for the home pregnancy kit, the one where you can grow the critter in an aquarium in your rec room—*in utero* pregnancies are strictly a drag. My other advice is, "Keep the poop talk to a minimum." While you might think that your single, childless friends are obligated to listen to detailed descriptions of your infant's bowel movements just because you often listened to blow-by-blow accounts of their hapless love affairs, remember: sex is always more interesting than defecation.

C. E. CRIMMINS

MUSIC

Never play a thing the same way twice.
LOUIS ARMSTRONG

Sometimes you have to play a long time to be able to play like yourself
MILES DAVIS

The wise musicians are those who play what they can master.
DUKE ELLINGTON

If we were all determined to play the first violin we should never have a full ensemble. Therefore respect every musician in his proper place.
ROBERT SCHUMANN

Playing the violin must be like making love—all or nothing.
ISAAC STERN

[Playing the cello] should be like singing to yourself.
MSTISLAV ROSTROPOVICH

Don't tap your foot—it makes your arms get tired.
THELONIOUS MONK to his bass player

Lean your body forward slightly to support the guitar against your chest, for the poetry of the music should resound in your heart.

ANDRÉS SEGOVIA

When the music business changed so drastically in the late sixties and rock began happening in such a big way, I went to Count Basie and said, "It's a complete takeover. What should I do?" Basie waited a beat, looked up at me with those big eyes of his, and said, "Why change an apple?"

TONY BENNETT

When in doubt, sing loud. ROBERT MERRILL

The softer you sing, the louder you're heard.

DONOVAN

Regard your voice as capital in the bank. . . . Sing on your interest and your voice will last.

LAURITZ MELCHIOR

You've got to find some way of saying it without saying it. DUKE ELLINGTON

○-○

You have to be Jewish.
                    RICHARD TUCKER to
                    Franco Corelli on how to sing Puccini

○-○

There are no wrong notes.   THELONIOUS MONK

        Music is your own experience—your thoughts,
        your wisdom. If you don't live it, it won't come
        out of your horn.   CHARLIE PARKER

○-○

When a piece gets difficult, makes faces.
                    ARTHUR SCHNABEL to Vladimir Horowitz

○-○

If you think you're boring your audience, go slower
not faster.   GUSTAV MAHLER

        In order to compose, all you need to do is remem-
        ber a tune that nobody else has thought of.
                                    ROBERT SCHUMANN

Want to be a composer? . . . If you can *think design,* you can *execute design*—it's only a bunch of air molecules, who's gonna check up on you? Just follow these simple instructions:

1. Declare your *intention* to create a "composition."

2. *Start* a piece at *some time.*

3. Cause *something to happen over a period of time* (it doesn't matter what happens in your "time hole"—we have critics to tell us whether it's any good or not, so we won't worry about that part).

4. *End the piece at some time* (or keep it going, telling the audience it is a "work in progress").

5. Get a part-time job so you can continue to do stuff like this. FRANK ZAPPA

o-o-o-o-o-o-o-o-o-o-o-o-o-o-o-o-o-o-o-o-o-o-o-o-o-o-o-o-o

Gioachino Rossini gave Richard Wagner this advice on how to deal with critics: "Answer them with silence and indifference. It works better, I assure you, than anger and argument. . . . Though you see me wearing a wig, I can assure you it wasn't those bumpkins who cost me a single hair of my head."

o-o-o-o-o-o-o-o-o-o-o-o-o-o-o-o-o-o-o-o-o-o-o-o-o-o-o-o-o

A symphony must be like the world. It must contain everything.   GUSTAV MAHLER

Composers should write tunes that chauffeurs and errand boys can whistle.   SIR THOMAS BEECHAM

Composers shouldn't think too much—it interferes with their plagiarism.   HOWARD DIETZ

Film music should have the same relationship to the film drama that somebody's piano playing in my living room has to the book I'm reading.
    IGOR STRAVINSKY

In a picture, the music should be heard and not seen.   MAX STEINER

Respectable people do not write music or make love as a career.   ALEXANDER BORODIN

Conductors must give unmistakable and suggestive signals to the orchestra—not choreography to the audience.   GEORGE SZELL

ON HOW TO PLAY

Accented notes: Like one shoe fits and the other is a little small.

A passage in Prokofiev: . . . like two bugs fighting.

Crescendo: . . . like a million devils.

Diminuendo: With expression—not like when you are turning radio down because neighbors complaining.

Sforzando: Four old women in audience must have heart attacks.

Tremolo: Like a hag who has false teeth and she is chewing caramels.

A Brahms variation: . . . like little crawling lousies.

Softly: Whisper like a lady moving in a silk dress.

MSTISLAV ROSTROPOVICH

○-○

First you go out and buy a stick—it's called a baton—about this long. Then you get some music, you get musicians together, you give them this music, you stand in front of them with the stick in your right hand, you go like this, and a mysterious thing happens: the musicians begin to play. Now, once the musicians are playing there are only two things you must remember, but they are very important: you must not disturb the musicians while they are playing, and second, when the musicians have stopped playing, you must stop conducting. SIGMUND ROMBERG

Never look at the brass . . . it only encourages them. RICHARD STRAUSS

In music one must think with the heart and feel with the brain. GEORGE SZELL

o-o-o-o-o-o-o-o-o-o-o-o-o-o-o-o-o-o-o-o-o-o-o-o-o-o-o-o-o-o-o-o-o-o-o

You have to play Mozart like Chopin and Chopin like Mozart. PABLO CASALS to Vladimir Horowitz

o-o-o-o-o-o-o-o-o-o-o-o-o-o-o-o-o-o-o-o-o-o-o-o-o-o-o-o-o-o-o-o-o-o-o

Always ask why you're doing anything. Be kind, especially if you have a gift. Be honest. Take risks. YO-YO MA

I've never known a musician who regretted being one. Whatever deceptions life may have in store for you, music itself is not going to let you down. VIRGIL THOMSON

You should never trust anyone who listens to Mahler before they're forty.　　CLIVE JAMES

You'll never make it—four-groups are out.
　　ANONYMOUS record company executive to
　　the Beatles, 1962

∘-∘

If you want to please only the critics, don't play too loud, too soft, too fast, too slow.
　　ARTURO TOSCANINI to Vladimir Horowitz

∘-∘

Don't try to join the "hit parade."　　PETE SEEGER

Go get a real estate license.　　FRANK ZAPPA

NEVER . . .

Never trust anyone over thirty.   JERRY RUBIN

Never underestimate the power of human stupidity.   ROBERT HEINLEIN

Never eat crackers in bed.   ANONYMOUS

Never get involved with someone who wants to change you.   QUENTIN CRISP

Never put off till tomorrow that which you can do today.   BENJAMIN FRANKLIN

Never do today what you can put off till tomorrow.   AARON BURR

Never put off until tomorrow what you can do the day after tomorrow.   MARK TWAIN

Never steal anything so small that you'll have to go to an unpleasant city jail for it instead of a minimum-security federal tennis prison.

P. J. O'ROURKE

Never send a man to do a horse's job. "MR. ED"

Never let anyone outside the family know what you're thinking.

> MARLON BRANDO in *The Godfather* (screenplay by Mario Puzo and Francis Ford Coppola)

Never be haughty to the humble. Never be humble to the haughty. JEFFERSON DAVIS

Never befriend the oppressed unless you are prepared to take on the oppressor. OGDEN NASH

Never lend books, for no one ever returns them; the only books I have in my library are books that other folks have lent to me.

> ANATOLE FRANCE

Never judge a book by its movie. J. W. EAGAN

Never try to make anyone like you: you know, and God knows, that one of you is enough.

> EMERSON

THREE NEVERS FOR PROPER GENTLEMEN

1. Never shoot south of the Thames.
2. Never follow whiskey with port.
3. Never have your wife in the morning—the day may have something better to offer. P. V. TAYLOR

Never economize on luxuries. ANGELA THIRKELL

Never give a sucker an even break.
W. C. FIELDS

Never keep shampoo in its original container— it's unsightly and commercial. JERRY ZIPKIN

Never take the antidote before the poison.
LATIN PROVERB

Never buy a thing you don't want merely because it is dear. OSCAR WILDE

Never run after your own hat—others will be delighted to do it; why spoil their fun?
MARK TWAIN

Never assume anything except a 4-¼ percent mortgage.   DAVE KINDRED

Never trust a man with short legs—brain's too near their bottoms.   NOEL COWARD

Never believe in mirrors or newspapers.
                                              JOHN OSBORNE

Never get out of bed before noon.
                                          CHARLES BUKOWSKI

Never slap a man who chews tobacco.
                                            WILLARD SCOTT

Never retreat. Never explain. Get it done and let them howl.   BENJAMIN JOWETT

Never fight an inanimate object. P. J. O'ROURKE

Never despise fashion. It's what we have instead of God.   MALCOLM BRADBURY

Never let your inferiors do you a favor—it will be extremely costly.   H. L. MENCKEN

Never insult an alligator until after you have crossed the river. CORDELL HULL

Never date a girl named "Ruby."   TOM WAITS

Never have yourself tattoed with any woman's name, not even her initials.   P. G. WODEHOUSE

Never offend people with style when you can offend them with substance.   TONY BROWN

Never co-sign.   AL McGUIRE

Never give a power-of-attorney.
DEBBIE REYNOLDS

Never put anything on paper . . . and never trust a man with a small black mustache.
P. G. WODEHOUSE

Never kick a fresh turd on a hot day.
HARRY S TRUMAN

Never walk if you can drive; and of two cigars, always choose the longest and strongest.
AUSTEN CHAMBERLAIN

Never get a mime talking. He won't stop.
MARCEL MARCEAU

Never underestimate a man who overestimates himself.
FRANKLIN D. ROOSEVELT

Never saw off the branch you are on, unless you are being hanged from it.
STANISLAW LEC

Never say anything on the phone that you wouldn't want your mother to hear at your trial.
SYDNEY BIDDLE BARROWS

Never jog while wearing wingtips—unless you are attending the Nerd Convention in Atlantic City.
MARK RUSSELL

Never put a razor inside your nose—even as a joke.
JAKE JOHANSEN

Never lend your car to anyone to whom you have given birth.
ERMA BOMBECK

Never drop your gun to hug a bear.
H. E. PALMER

Never thank anybody for anything, except a drink of water in the desert—and then make it brief.
GENE FOWLER

Never give in, never, never, never, never.
WINSTON CHURCHILL

Being a politician is like being a football coach: you have to be small enough to understand the game, but dumb enough to think it's important.
EUGENE MCCARTHY

The biggest danger for a politician is to shake hands with a man who is physically stronger, has been drinking, and is voting for the other guy.
WILLIAM PROXMIRE

When you're leading, don't talk.
THOMAS E. DEWEY

Meet the sun every day as if it could cast a ballot.
HENRY CABOT LODGE, JR., to novice political campaigner Dwight D. Eisenhower

Don't try to take on a new personality; it doesn't work.
RICHARD NIXON

If your opponent calls you a liar, call him a thief.
"BIG BILL" THOMPSON

Look over your shoulder now and then to be sure someone's following you.　　HENRY GILMER

A cardinal rule of politics: never get caught in bed with a live man or a dead woman.
LARRY HAGMAN as J. R. Ewing in *Dallas*

It is dangerous for a national candidate to say things that people might remember.
EUGENE MCCARTHY

○-○

HOW TO HANDLE THE MEDIA

No matter how many friends he may think he has in the press . . . the president must recognize that his relationship with the media is primarily adversarial. TV reporters always claim to be "speaking for the people," but they are really speaking for themselves. In many ways they are political actors just like the president, mindful of their ratings, careful of preserving and building their power. A president must respect them for that power, but he can never entirely trust them.   RICHARD NIXON

The most guileful among the reporters . . . are those who appear friendly and smile and seem to be supportive. They are the ones who seek to gut you on every occasion.
EDWARD KOCH

Reporters are not required to read you your Miranda rights.   CHRISTOPHER MATTHEWS

Never tell a lie to a reporter; everyone I've seen do it has gotten in a helluva lot of trouble.   JOSEPH CALIFANO

If you lose your temper at a newspaper columnist, he'll get rich or famous or both.   JAMES C. HAGERTY

Practice whatever the big truth is so that you can say it in forty seconds on camera.   NEWT GINGRICH

In dealing with the press do yourself a favor. Stick with one of three responses: (a) I know and I can tell you; (b) I know and I can't tell you; or (c) I don't know.
DAN RATHER

Colonel, never go out to meet trouble. If you will just sit still, nine cases out of ten someone will intercept it before it reaches you.

CALVIN COOLIDGE to Theodore Roosevelt

If you have a weak candidate and a weak platform, wrap yourself up in the American flag and talk about the Constitution.   MATTHEW S. QUAY

Stand not too near the rich man lest he destroy thee—and not too far away lest he forget thee.

ANEURIN BEVAN

If you're running against Nixon you don't have to say *anything*. You don't even have to get out of bed in the morning to beat him.

HARRY S. TRUMAN advising Edmund "Pat" Brown to keep his speeches short in his campaign for the governorship of California against Richard Nixon.

Always stay in with the outs.

DAVID HALBERSTAM

> You have to give the electorate a tune they can whistle.   ENOCH POWELL

Don't put no restrictions on the people. Leave 'em the hell alone.   JIMMY DURANTE

∘-∘

1. When the polls are in your favor, flaunt them.
2. When the polls are overwhelmingly unfavorable,
   (a) ridicule and dismiss them, or
   (b) stress the volatility of public opinion.

3. When the polls are slightly unfavorable, play for sympathy as a struggling underdog.

4. When too close to call, be surprised at your own strength.   PAUL DICKSON

∘-∘

> Don't worry about polls, but if you do, don't admit it.   ROSALYNN CARTER

Never participate in anything without consulting the American Legion or your local Chamber of Commerce.   MARTIN DIES

It is always best and safest to count on nothing from the Americans but words.

NEVILLE CHAMBERLAIN

Americans are big boys. You can talk them into almost anything. Sit with them for half an hour over a bottle of whiskey and be a nice guy.

NGUYEN CAO KY

The Jews and Arabs should settle their dispute in the true spirit of Christian charity.

ALEXANDER WILEY

There are three roads to ruin: women, gambling, and technicians. The most pleasant is with women, the quickest is with gambling, but the surest is with technicians.

GEORGES POMPIDOU

If you're going to plagiarize, go *way* back.

SENATOR BARRY GOLDWATER
to Senator Joseph Biden

To lead the people, walk behind them. LAO-TZU

I would advise anyone who wished to obtain a favor from a minister to approach him with a mournful air rather than a lighthearted one. No one likes to see those who are happier than himself. NICOLAS CHAMFORT

When you are smashing monuments, save the pedestals—they always come in handy.
STANISLAW LEC

If you take yourself seriously in politics, you've had it. LORD CARRINGTON

Never murder a man when he's busy committing suicide. WOODROW WILSON

You can fool too many of the people too much of the time. JAMES THURBER

If you feed the people with revolutionary slogans they will listen today, they will listen tomorrow, they will listen the day after tomorrow, but on the fourth day they will say, "To hell with you."
NIKITA KHRUSHCHEV

The United States and the Soviet Union reached the brink of nuclear war during the Cuban Missile Crisis in October of 1962. With an American naval blockade on Soviet shipping and American forces poised to attack the island of Cuba, the U.S. received two conflicting cables from Soviet General Secretary Nikita Khrushchev. The first message offered removal of Soviet missiles from Cuba in return for a U.S. promise not to attempt another invasion, but the second message, which reached Washington several hours later, demanded that in return for the removal of Soviet missiles from Cuba, the U.S. should remove its missiles from Turkey. Robert F. Kennedy, the attorney general and one of President John F. Kennedy's most trusted advisors, suggested that the president ignore the latter telegram and respond to the former. President Kennedy took his brother's advice: the ploy worked, the missiles were removed, and World War III was averted.

If you want to get along, go along.

SAM RAYBURN

If you can't stand the heat, stay out of the kitchen.
HARRY S TRUMAN

If you have to eat crow, eat it while it's hot.
ALBEN W. BARKLEY

If you can't deliver the pie in the sky you promised, you'd better redefine the pie.
PAUL A. SAMUELSON

He who slings mud generally loses ground.
ADLAI STEVENSON

Once you pledge, don't hedge.
NIKITA KHRUSHCHEV

When a man has to make a speech, the first thing he has to decide is what to say.   GERALD FORD

If you have an important point to make, don't try to be subtle or clever. Use a pile driver. Hit the point once. Then come back and hit it again. Then hit it a third time—a tremendous whack.
WINSTON CHURCHILL

The oilcan is mightier than the sword.
EVERETT DIRKSEN

A little vagueness goes a long way in this business.
EDMUND G. "PAT" BROWN, JR.

If you can't convince them, confuse them.
HARRY S TRUMAN

The best audience is intelligent, well-educated, and a little drunk.
ALBEN W. BARKLEY

o-o-o-o-o-o-o-o-o-o-o-o-o-o-o-o-o-o-o-o-o-o-o-o-o-o-o-o-o-o-o-o-o-o

During the 1964 Presidential campaign, Republican candidate Barry Goldwater put his foot in his mouth again and again, prompting members of his campaign staff to advise reporters, "Don't quote what he says, say what he means."

o-o-o-o-o-o-o-o-o-o-o-o-o-o-o-o-o-o-o-o-o-o-o-o-o-o-o-o-o-o-o-o-o-o

A candidate for office can have no greater advantage than muddled syntax; no greater liability than a command of the language.
MARYA MANNES

Senators are a prolific source of advice, and most of it is bad. DEAN ACHESON

You can't use tact with a congressman. A congressman is a hog. You must take a stick and hit him on the snout. HENRY ADAMS

The first requirement of a statesman is that he be dull. This is not always easy to achieve.
DEAN ACHESON

You can always get the truth from an American statesman after he has turned seventy, or given up all hope of the presidency.
WENDELL PHILLIPS

You really have to be careful of politicians who have no further ambitions: they may run for the presidency. HARRY S TRUMAN

One of the first lessons a president has to learn is that every word he says weighs a ton.
CALVIN COOLIDGE

The president has so much good publicity potential that hasn't been exploited. He should just sit down one day and make a list of all the things that people are embarrassed to do that they shouldn't be embarrassed to do, and then do them all on television.   ANDY WARHOL

◇-◇

There are no easy matters that will come to you as president. If they are easy they will be settled at a lower level.
            DWIGHT D. EISENHOWER to John F. Kennedy

◇-◇

Whenever I was upset by something in the papers, [Jack] always told me to be more tolerant, like a horse flicking away flies in the summer.
                        JACQUELINE KENNEDY

◇-◇

LBJ'S POLITICAL PRIMER

Better to have [your political enemies] inside the tent pissin' out than outside pissin' in.

Hug your friends tight, but your enemies tighter—hug 'em so tight they can't wiggle.

While you're savin' your face, you're losin' your ass.

If you have a mother-in-law with only one eye and she has it in the center of her forehead, you don't keep her in the living room.

Eisenhower told me never to trust a communist.

Never trust a man unless you've got his pecker in your pocket.

If you can't raise money in your own state you're in trouble.

If you're in politics and you can't tell when you walk into a room who's for you and who's against you, then you're in the wrong line of work.

You never want to give a man a present when he's feeling good. You want to do it when he's down.

When things haven't gone well for you, call in a secretary or a staff man and chew him out. You will sleep better and they will appreciate the attention.

LYNDON BAINES JOHNSON

o-o-o-o-o-o-o-o-o-o-o-o-o-o-o-o-o-o-o-o-o-o-o-o-o-o-o-o-o-o-o-o-o-o-o-o

Don't jump on a man unless he's down.

FINLEY PETER DUNNE

If you can't carry your own precinct you're in trouble.

CALVIN COOLIDGE

If you're going to sin, sin against God, not the bureaucracy. God will forgive you but the bureaucracy won't.

HYMAN RICKOVER

o-o-o-o-o-o-o-o-o-o-o-o-o-o-o-o-o-o-o-o-o-o-o-o-o-o-o-o-o-o-o-o-o-o-o-o-o

GUIDELINES FOR BUREAUCRATS

1. When in charge, ponder.
2. When in trouble, delegate.
3. When in doubt, mumble.

JAMES H. BOREN

o-o-o-o-o-o-o-o-o-o-o-o-o-o-o-o-o-o-o-o-o-o-o-o-o-o-o-o-o-o-o-o-o-o-o-o-o

Every government is run by liars and nothing they say should be believed.

I. F. STONE

A government that robs Peter to pay Paul can always depend upon the support of Paul.

GEORGE BERNARD SHAW

o-o-o-o-o-o-o-o-o-o-o-o-o-o-o-o-o-o-o-o-o-o-o-o-o-o-o-o-o-o-o-o-o-o

You better take advantage of the good cigars. You don't get much else in that job.

> THOMAS P. "TIP" O'NEILL to Vice President
> Walter Mondale

o-o-o-o-o-o-o-o-o-o-o-o-o-o-o-o-o-o-o-o-o-o o o o-o-o-o-o-u-u-o-o-o-o-o-o-o-o

When someone with a rural accent says, "I don't know anything about politics," zip up your pockets.   DONALD RUMSFELD

> In politics, if you want anything said, ask a man;
> if you want anything done, ask a woman.
>   MARGARET THATCHER

It's a good rule to follow the first law of holes: if you are in one, stop digging.   DENIS HEALEY

o-o-o-o-o-o-o-o-o-o-o-o-o-o-o-o-o-o-o-o-o-o-o-o-o-o-o-o-o-o-o-o-o-o

Stop looking at the world through rose-colored bifocals.
> DOROTHY PARKER to a right-wing reactionary

o-o-o-o-o-o-o-o-o-o-o-o-o-o-o-o-o-o-o-o-o-o-o-o-o-o-o-o-o-o-o-o-o-o

Whenever you find that you are on the side of the majority, it is time to reform (or pause and reflect). MARK TWAIN

A politician's willingness to listen to advice rises in inverse proportion to how badly he thinks he is doing. PAT CADDELL

On a throne at the center of a sense of humor sits a capacity for irony. All wit rests on a cheerful awareness of life's incongruities. It is a gentling awareness, and no politician without it should be allowed near power. GEORGE WILL

ADVERTISING EXECUTIVES

The guy you've really got to reach with your advertising is the copywriter for your chief rival's advertising agency. If you can terrorize him, you've got it licked.   HOWARD GOSSAGE

> When the client moans and sighs
> Make his logo twice the size.
> When the client's hopping mad,
> Put his picture in the ad.
> If he still should prove refractory
> Add a picture of his factory.
>   ANONYMOUS

○-○

Robert Benchley worked in the advertising department of Curtis Publishing Company—briefly: "When I left Curtis (I was given plenty of time to get my hat and coat) I was advised not to stick to advertising. They said I was too tall, or something."

○-○

ANTHROPOLOGISTS

The way to do field work is never to come up for
air until it is all over.   MARGARET MEAD

ARCHITECTS

No house should ever be *on* any hill or anything.
It should be *of* the hill, so hill and house can live
together each the happier for the other.
                              FRANK LLOYD WRIGHT

BRITISH COLONIAL OFFICERS

Never touch hard liquor till the sun goes down,
and never go to bed quite sober.   HILARY HOOK

CLERGYMEN

A bishop ought to die on his legs.
                    JOHN WOOLTON, Bishop of Exeter

If you're ever being chased by a crocodile, run in
a zigzag pattern because they can only run fast
on a straightaway.
          FATHER GUIDO SARDUCCI (DON NOVELLO)

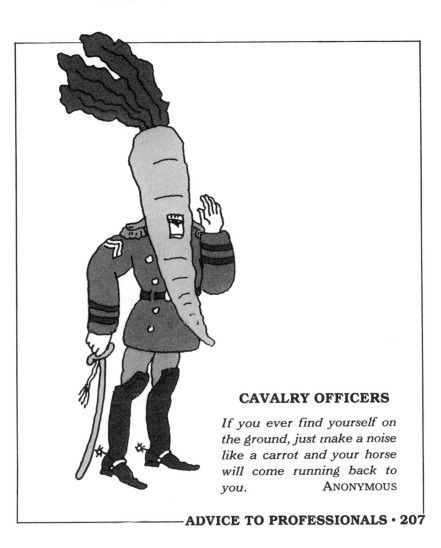

CAVALRY OFFICERS

If you ever find yourself on the ground, just make a noise like a carrot and your horse will come running back to you. ANONYMOUS

CRITICS

The reader deserves an honest opinion. If he doesn't deserve it, give it to him anyhow.

JOHN CIARDI

You shouldn't say it is not good. You should say you do not like it; and then . . . you're perfectly safe. JAMES McNEILL WHISTLER

DANCERS

Think of the magic of that foot, comparatively small, upon which your whole weight rests. It's a miracle, and the dance . . . is a celebration of that miracle. MARTHA GRAHAM

A good education is usually harmful to a dancer. A good calf is better than a good head.

AGNES DE MILLE

DIPLOMATS

One of the best ways to persuade others is with your ears—by listening. DEAN RUSK

To make a good salad is to be a brilliant diplomatist—the problem is entirely the same in both cases. To know exactly how much oil one must put with one's vinegar. OSCAR WILDE

My advice to any diplomat who wants to have a good press is to have two or three kids and a dog.
CARL ROWAN

Above all, do not fail to give good dinners, and pay attention to the women.
NAPOLEON BONAPARTE

FOOTMEN

While waiting at dinner, never be picking your nose, or scratching your head, or any other part of your body; neither blow your nose in the room; if you have a cold, and cannot help doing it, do it on the outside of the door; but do not sound your nose like a trumpet, that all the house may hear you when you blow it; still it is better to blow your nose when it requires, than to be picking it and snuffing up the mucus, which is a filthy trick.
T. COSNETT

GRAND PRIX DRIVERS

It is necessary to relax your muscles whenever you can. Relaxing your brain is fatal.

STIRLING MOSS

GUNFIGHTERS

Never run away from a gun. Bullets can travel faster than you can. Besides, if you're going to be hit, you had better get it in the front than in the back. It looks better.   WILD BILL HICKOCK

HEADMASTERS

Work 'em hard, play 'em hard, feed 'em up to the nines, and send 'em to bed so tired that they are asleep before their heads are on the pillow.

FRANK L. BOYDEN,
Headmaster, Deerfield Academy

HORSE TRAINERS

It can be set down in four words: the best of everything. The best hay, oats, and water.

JAMES "SUNNY JIM" FITZSIMMONS

HUMORISTS

Wit ought to be a glorious treat, like caviar; never spread it around like marmalade. NOEL COWARD

Words with a *k* in them are funny. If it doesn't have a *k*, it's not funny. NEIL SIMON

To all aspiring young comedians—when are you going to do something with your life? Get a real job in hardware sales or taxidermy—meet a nice girl, settle down, and stop hanging around those comedy clubs with all your comedy bum friends. Your mother and I slaved and scrimped and you— (sorry, I got carried away). Okay, if you are really serious about being a comedian, stay away from politics. This is too precious a government and our politicians are above reproach and undeserving of any lack of respect on your part. Better yet—people love jokes about badminton.

MARK RUSSELL

Never perform for other comedians, perform for the audience. DANNY THOMAS

Don't do blue.   RED SKELTON

○-○

Young comedians: first of all, be honest with yourself. Are you truly malcontented, or merely bitter? Malcontent is an aesthetic state, while bitterness is a state reserved for the thwarted upwardly mobile. I like to think I'm a malcontent, but I'm afraid I may be merely bitter.

If you are truly malcontented, you won't heed my advice anyway. You'll think to yourself, "A lot he knows," or "What gives this jerk the right to tell me what to do?" and you'll go off by yourself and drink heavily or glower at photographs of old girlfriends. If you're bitter, on the other hand, you'll say the same thing, but you'll steal my advice, try to fob it off as your own, come to believe it *is* your own, and when people reject your advice, you'll drink heavily or glower at photographs of old girlfriends. So the distinction is subtle.

I don't have much to offer in the way of advice.

1. Don't say bad things about Elvis.

If you do harbor bad feelings about Elvis, keep them to yourself. Fans of Elvis don't want to hear it, and nobody else cares.

2. Avoid politics, if you can.

I'm assuming you want to make humor your profession. That Dan Quayle joke you're playing with? Somewhere in America, that very same joke is being told at a water cooler. Why waste your time? You can make fun of liberals, but it's kind of like kicking a three-legged dog. And making fun of conservatives is a waste of time, because they have no sense of humor. Conservatives call jokes "japeries" or "jests." You could probably get a chuckle out of a conservative, but it would have to be a pun in Latin about Edmund Burke. This will not make you any money. Stick with the tried-and-true sources of humor, which are (1) how terrible Chinese drivers are, (2) how hard it is to have sex these days what with AIDS and women's lib and all, (3) how terrible television commercials are, (4) how terrible fast food is, and (5) how much you hate Los Angeles.

3. Get a job, kid.

MERLE KESSLER (a.k.a. IAN SHOALES)

INTERVIEWERS

Wait for those unguarded moments. Relax the mood, and, like the child dropping off to sleep, the subject often reveals his truest self.

BARBARA WALTERS

LABOR NEGOTIATORS

The trick is to be there when it's settled.

ARTHUR GOLDBERG

MAFIOSI

Never get angry, never make a threat. Reason with people.

MARLON BRANDO in *The Godfather*
(screenplay by Mario Puzo
and Francis Ford Coppola)

Don't carry a gun. It's nice to have them close by, but don't carry them. You might get arrested.

JOHN GOTTI

Always eat a large breakfast; never try to cheat on your taxes.

FRANK COSTELLO

Keep a neat appearance at all times.

BENJAMIN RUGGIERO

MAGAZINE EDITORS/PUBLISHERS

1. Find a niche that allows you to pursue a personal passion.

2. Test your idea to make sure you've identified a market, not just a need.

3. Say goodbye to family and friends—you won't see much of them for two or three years.

4. Dive in, be prepared to fail, be prepared to succeed, be willing to change course.

5. Consider learning a real craft, or getting a real job.   ERIC UTNE

He who edits least edits best. ARNOLD GINGRICH

Number your magazine pages consecutively!
                                      WILLIAM M. GAINES

METEOROLOGISTS

Looking out the window is the most important thing if you want to know what's going on.
                HAROLD M. GIBSON, U.S. Weather Bureau

PHYSICIANS

There is only one cardinal rule: one must always *listen* to the patient.   DR. OLIVER SACKS

POLICE

You want to make a guy comfortable enough to confess to murder.

BILL CLARK, Brooklyn Detective

PRIZE FIGHTERS

Float like a butterfly, sting like a bee.

DREW BUNDINI BROWN

If you ever get belted and see three fighters through a haze, go after the one in the middle. That's what ruined me—I went after the two guys on the end.   MAX BAER

◦-◦

The hero and the coward both feel the same thing, but the hero uses his fear, projects it onto his opponent, while the coward runs. It's the same thing, fear, but it's what you do with it that matters.

CUS D'AMATO to Mike Tyson

◦-◦

PRODUCERS

Never take any one man's opinion as final. Never take your own opinion as final. Never expect anyone to help you but yourself.

IRVING THALBERG

Anybody who has taste is a producer. That is all you have to have, with a little bit of ability. If you can be a producer without taste, you have to have money. You have to have one or the other. Also, it is nice to have some kind of heft. You can also have a piece of property. That will give you heft. You can say, "I just bought all of Joseph Conrad's manuscripts, all of the unpublished ones." That will give you heft until they say, "Who is Joseph Conrad?" That's when you've got no heft. But many things can give you heft. One successful production will give you heft. An attitude will give you heft. Also, you can have heft if you are a very smart guy who knows what you are doing.

CARL REINER

Learn to read. DAVID BROWN

PROMOTERS

The only promotion rules I can think of are that a sense of shame is to be avoided at all costs and there is never any reason for a hustler to be less cunning to more virtuous men. Oh yes . . . whenever you think you've got something really great, add ten percent more.   BILL VEECK

Don't try to explain it, just sell it.
                              COLONEL TOM PARKER

SALESPERSONS

When you stop talking, you've lost your customer. When you turn your back, you've lost her.
                              ESTEE LAUDER

SANTA CLAUSES

Santa is even-tempered. Santa does not hit children over the head who kick him. Santa uses the term *folks* rather than *Mommy and Daddy* because of all the broken homes. Santa does not have a three-martini lunch. Santa does not borrow money from store employees. Santa wears a good deodorant.   JENNY ZINK

RESTAURATEURS

*The best way to launch an Italian restaurant is to have it
raided because the Mafia eats there. Everybody knows
they eat well.* MARIO PUZO

ADVICE TO PROFESSIONALS · 219

SCIENTISTS

It is a good morning exercise for a research scientist to discard a pet hypothesis every day before breakfast. It keeps him young. KONRAD LORENZ

> I cannot give any scientist of any age better advice than this: the intensity of a conviction that a hypothesis is true has no bearing over whether it is true or not.   PETER MEDAWAR

Concern for man and his fate must always form the chief interest of all technical endeavors. . . . Never forget this in the midst of your diagrams and equations.   ALBERT EINSTEIN

> Never look at data on a Friday night. It can spoil your weekend.   ANONYMOUS RESEARCHER

SET DESIGNERS

Be daring, be different, be impractical; be anything that will assert integrity of purpose and imaginative vision against the play-it-safers, the creatures of the commonplace, the slaves of the ordinary. Routines have their purposes, but the merely routine is the hidden enemy of high art.

CECIL BEATON

SPIES

To betray, you must first belong.

HAROLD "KIM" PHILBY

○-○

HOW TO SPREAD A RUMOR

1. Tell the story casually, and don't give yourself away by being overanxious to launch your rumor.

2. If the lowdown is especially hot, tell it confidentially.

3. Never speak your rumor more than once in the same place. If it is good, others will repeat it.

4. Tell it innocently, and don't disclose any source that can readily be discredited.

BRITISH MORALE OPERATIONS SECTION
to Burmese agents during World War II

○-○

When you break into a man's office, you should always make it a point to steal something.

JACK LORD as Steve McGarrett
in *Hawaii Five-0*

SURGEONS

Never say "oops" in the operating room.

DR. LEO TROY

TEACHERS

The teacher should never lose his temper in the presence of the class. If a man, he may take refuge in profane soliloquies; if a woman, she may follow the example of one sweet-faced and apparently tranquil girl—go out in the yard and gnaw a post.   WILLIAM LYON PHELPS

> Don't try to fix the students, fix ourselves first. The good teacher makes the poor student good and the good student superior. When our students fail, we, as teachers too, have failed.
>
> MARVA COLLINS

Make a kid feel stupid and he'll act stupider.

JOHN HOLT

Though thou canst not forebear to love, forebear
to link.   SIR WALTER RALEIGH

> Contraceptives should be used on every conceiv-
> able occasion.   SPIKE MILLIGAN

The best contraceptive is the word *no*—repeated
frequently.   MARGARET SMITH

> A wise woman never yields by appointment.
>   STENDHAL

It doesn't matter what you do in the bedroom as
long as you don't do it in the street and frighten
the horses.   MRS. PATRICK CAMPBELL

> Lie back and think of England.
>   ANONYMOUS Victorian advice to women

Sex is a pleasurable exercise in plumbing, but be
careful or you'll get yeast in your drain tap.
                                   RITA MAE BROWN

In the case of some women, orgasms take quite a bit of time. Before signing on with such a partner, make sure you are willing to lay aside, say, the month of June, with sandwiches having to be brought it.   BRUCE JAY FRIEDMAN

Sleeping alone, except under doctor's orders, does much harm. Children will tell you how lonely it is sleeping alone. If possible you should always sleep with someone you love. You recharge your mutual batteries free of charge.

MARLENE DIETRICH

I think you should always laugh in bed—people always laugh at me when I'm in bed.

BOY GEORGE

The next time you feel the desire [to masturbate] coming on, don't give way to it. If you have the chance, just wash your parts in cold water and cool them down.

ROBERT BADEN-POWELL to Boy Scouts

Never let the little head do the thinking for the big head.   ANONYMOUS advice to teenage boys

Going to bed with a woman never hurt a ballplayer. It's staying up all night looking for them that does you in.

CASEY STENGEL

Too much of a good thing is wonderful.

MAE WEST

To succeed with the opposite sex, tell her you're impotent. She can't wait to disprove it.

CARY GRANT

o-o-o-o-o-o-o-o-o-o-o-o-o-o-o-o-o-o-o-o-o-o-o-o-o-o-o-o-o-o-o-o-o

Ernest Hemingway advised the poet Allen Tate to ration his sexual encounters because, Hemingway explained, the number of ejaculations allotted to each man is fixed at birth. Balzac dispensed the same advice based on his belief that sperm and brain matter were one and the same and that every orgasm spent creative power. And Leo Tolstoy said that his Aunt Toinette, with whom he lived after being orphaned at the age of nine, always told him to have an affair with a married woman. "There is no better education than an affair with a woman of good breeding," she advised him.

o-o-o-o-o-o-o-o-o-o-o-o-o-o-o-o-o-o-o-o-o-o-o-o-o-o-o-o-o-o-o-o-o

Jump out the window if you are the object of passion. Flee it if you feel it. . . . Passion goes, boredom remains.   COCO CHANEL

Anything worth doing well is worth doing slowly.
                    GYPSY ROSE LEE

SUCCESS

If at first you don't succeed, you may be at your
level of incompetence already.

> LAURENCE J. PETER

If at first you do succeed—try to hide your aston-
ishment.   HARRY F. BANKS

To be successful you have to be lucky, or a little
mad, or very talented, or to find yourself in a
rapid-growth field.   EDWARD DE BONO

If you want to win anything—a race, your self,
your life—you have to go a little berserk.

> GEORGE SHEEHAN

There's nothing to winning, really. That is, if you
happen to be blessed with a keen eye, an agile
mind, and no scruples whatsoever.

> ALFRED HITCHCOCK

Everything comes to him who hustles while he
waits.   THOMAS A. EDISON

Don't complain, don't explain.   HENRY FORD II

> Nothing succeeds like the appearance of success.
> CHRISTOPHER LASCH

Nothing succeeds like address.   FRAN LEBOWITZ

> You can have anything you want if you want it
> desperately enough. You must want it with an
> inner exuberance that erupts through the skin
> and joins the energy that created the world.
> SHEILA GRAHAM

If you can't keep up, drag them down to your
level.   LAURENCE J. PETER

> It is better for one's reputation to fail convention-
> ally than to succeed unconventionally.
> JOHN MAYNARD KEYNES

If a man keeps his trap shut, the world will beat a
path to his door.   FRANKLIN P. ADAMS

> When your work speaks for itself, don't interrupt.
> HENRY J. KAISER

You can get much further with a kind word and a gun than you can with a kind word alone.   AL CAPONE

An ounce of hypocrisy is worth a pound of ambition.
MICHAEL KORDA

By working faithfully eight hours a day you may eventually get to be boss and work twelve hours a day.
ROBERT FROST

Success *is* all it's cracked up to be. Life gets better, the work is nicer, and I'm nicer.
DANIEL TRAVANTI

The best way to make your dreams come true is to wake up.
PAUL VALÉRY

Things may come to those who wait, but only the things left by those who hustle.
ABRAHAM LINCOLN

The classic formula for success is: "Dress British, Think Yiddish."
OLD ADAGE

Appearances count: get a sun lamp . . . maintain an elegant address even if you live in the attic; patronize posh watering holes even if you have to

nurse your drink. Never niggle when you're short
of cash.   ARISTOTLE ONASSIS

The avocation of assessing the failures of better
men can be turned into a comfortable livelihood,
providing you back it up with a Ph.D.

NELSON ALGREN

I know very little about Washington University
beyond the fact that there are on its faculty . . .
excellent poets—William Gass, Stanley Elkin,
Howard Nemerov, and Mona Van Duyn—all of
whom are reported to be fine teachers as well.
Enroll in their course before you graduate. As
they are also quite famous, hit them for letters of
recommendation for your job-placement files, and
you'll be a shoo-in to graduate school if that is
whither you incline. But do this only after you
have done brilliant, even astonishing work in their
courses; otherwise take your C and don't be pushy.

JOHN BARTH

There's a standard formula for success in the
entertainment medium, and that is: "Beat it to
death if it succeeds."   ERNIE KOVACS

To succeed in the world it is not enough to be stupid, you must also be well-mannered.

VOLTAIRE

People will accept your idea much more readily if you tell them Benjamin Franklin said it first.

DAVID H. COMINS

The best way to get on in the world is to make people believe it's to their advantage to help you.

LA BRUYÈRE

The secret to success is to offend the greatest number of people.   GEORGE BERNARD SHAW

Always listen to experts. They'll tell you what can't be done and why. Then do it.

ROBERT HEINLEIN

A man must have a certain amount of intelligent ignorance to get anywhere.

CHARLES F. KETTERING

There is the greatest practical benefit in making a few failures early in life.   T. H. HUXLEY

I owe my success to having listened respectfully to the very best advice, and then going away and doing the exact opposite.   G. K. CHESTERTON

I was trying to think the other day about what you do now in America if you want to be successful. Before, you were dependable and wore a good suit. Looking around, I guess that today you have to do all the same things but not wear a good suit. I guess that's all it is. Think rich. Look poor.   ANDY WARHOL

Eighty percent of success is showing up.
    WOODY ALLEN

Rise early. Work late. Strike oil. J. PAUL GETTY

The key is not the "will to win" . . . everybody has that. It is the will to *prepare* to win that is important.   BOBBY KNIGHT

Keep your head up; act like a champion.
              PAUL "BEAR" BRYANT

If you aren't fired with enthusiasm, you'll be fired with enthusiasm.   VINCE LOMBARDI

If there's one pitch you keep swinging at and keep missing, stop swinging at it.   YOGI BERRA

Be quick, but never hurry.   JOHN WOODEN

You never get ahead of anyone as long as you try to get even with him.   LOU HOLTZ

You can't win all the time. There are guys out there who are better than you.   YOGI BERRA

If you make every game a life-and-death proposition, you're going to have problems. For one thing, you'll be dead a lot.   DEAN SMITH

A little bit of perfume doesn't hurt you if you don't drink it.   DARRELL ROYAL

Publicity is like poison: it doesn't hurt unless you swallow it.   JOE PATERNO

It's what you learn after you know it all that counts.   JOHN WOODEN

○-○ ○ ○

As a teenager the actor Timothy Hutton attended a basketball camp run by the legendary UCLA coach John Wooden. Hutton waited all week for a chance to talk to the "Wizard of Westwood," and he finally got his chance when, on the last day of camp, he spotted Wooden standing alone watching a workout. "Is there anything you can tell me that will help me be a success?" Hutton asked timidly. "Get a haircut," replied Wooden.

○-○

Breaks balance out. The sun don't shine on the same ol' dog's ass every day.   DARRELL ROYAL

You play the way you practice.   POP WARNER

If you don't get it by midnight, chances are you ain't gonna get it; and if you do, it ain't worth it.
CASEY STENGEL

Trade a player a year too early rather than a year too late.   BRANCH RICKEY

You've got to be in position for luck to happen. Luck doesn't go around looking for a stumble-bum.   DARRELL ROYAL

A winner never whines.   PAUL BROWN

You really never lose until you stop trying.
MIKE DITKA

Win any way you can as long as you can get away with it.   LEO DUROCHER

If you're old and you lose, they say you're outmoded. If you're young and you lose, they say you're green. So don't lose.   TERRY BRENNAN

You're gonna lose some ballgames and you're gonna win some ballgames and that's about it.
SPARKY ANDERSON

You don't save a pitcher for tomorrow. Tomorrow it may rain.   LEO DUROCHER

Play like you've got guts coming out of your ears.
PAUL "BEAR" BRYANT

Like my old skleenball coach used to say, "Find out what you don't do well, then don't do it."
"ALF"

TRAVEL

To feel at home, stay at home. A foreign country is not designed to make you comfortable. It's designed to make its own people comfortable.

CLIFTON FADIMAN

Whenever possible, avoid airlines which have anyone's first name in their titles, like Bob's International Airline or Air Fred. "MISS PIGGY"

The wise traveler [to Beirut] will pack shirts or blouses with ample breast pockets. Reaching inside a jacket for your passport looks too much like going for the draw and puts armed men out of countinence.

P. J. O'ROURKE

In an underdeveloped country, don't drink the water; in a developed country, don't breathe the air.

CHANGING TIMES MAGAZINE

Never trust anything you read in a travel article. Travel articles appear in publications that sell large, expensive advertisements to tourism-related industries, and these industries do not wish to see articles with headlines like: URUGUAY: DON'T BOTHER.   DAVE BARRY

One of the special beauties of America is that it is the only country in the world where you are not advised to learn the language before entering. Before I ever set out for the United States, I asked a friend if I should study American. His answer was unequivocal. "On no account," he said. "The more English you sound, the more likely you are to be believed."   QUENTIN CRISP

Things on the whole are much faster in America; people don't *stand for election*, they *run for office*. If a person say she's *sick,* it doesn't mean regurgitating, it means *ill. Mad* means angry, not insane. Don't ask for left-luggage; it's called a checkroom. A nice joint means a good pub, not roast meat.
                                        JESSICA MITFORD

Never play peek-a-boo with a child on a long plane trip. There's no end to the game. Finally I grabbed him by the bib and said, "Look, it's always gonna be me!"   RITA RUDNER

When you're on a sleeper at night, take your pocketbook and put it in a sock under your pillow. That way, the next morning you won't forget your pocketbook 'cause you'll be looking for your sock. PING BODIE

Whenever I travel I like to keep the seat next to me empty. I found a great way to do it. When someone walks down the aisle and says to you, "Is someone sitting there?" just say, "No one—except the Lord." CAROL LEIFER

○-○

As my good friend Al Capp told me a few years ago, the best thing to do with a confirmed [hotel] reservation slip when you have no room is to spread it out on the sidewalk in front of the hotel and go to sleep on it. You'll either embarrass the hotel into giving you a room or you'll be hauled off to the local jug, where at least you'll have a roof over your head. ART BUCHWALD

○-○

Dress impressively like the French, speak with authority like the Germans, have blond hair like the Scandinavians, and speak of no American presidents except, Lincoln, Roosevelt, and Kennedy.   SYLVAINE ROUY NEVES

Never learn to do anything: if you don't learn, you'll always find someone else to do it for you.

Be careless in your dress if you will, but keep a tidy soul.

Don't go around saying the world owes you a living; the world owes you nothing, it was here first.

Have a place for everything and keep the thing somewhere else; this is not a piece of advice, it is merely a custom.

It's a good idea to obey all the rules when you're young just so you'll have the strength to break them when you're old.

Grief can take care of itself, but to get the full value of joy you must have somebody to divide it with.

Always obey your superiors—if you have any.

In certain trying circumstances, urgent circumstances, desperate circumstances, profanity furnishes a relief denied even to prayer.

There are several good protections against temptation, but the surest is cowardice.

Never tell the truth to people who are not worthy of it.

Too much of anything is bad, but too much of good whiskey is barely enough.

We ought never to do wrong when people are looking.

Let us not be too particular: it is better to have old secondhand diamonds than none at all.

Do something every day that you don't want to do; this is the golden rule for acquiring the habit of doing your duty without pain.

If a person offend you, and you are in doubt as to whether it was intentional or not, do not resort to extreme measures; simply watch your chance and hit him with a brick.

If you tell the truth you don't have to remember anything.

Always acknowledge a fault frankly. This will throw those in authority off their guard and give you an opportunity to commit more.

Always do right. This will gratify some people and astonish the rest.

All you need to be assured of success in this life is ignorance and confidence.

There is no use in your walking five miles to fish when you can depend on being just as unsuccessful near home.

Part of the secret of success in life is to eat what you like and let the food fight it out inside.

When angry, count four; when very angry, swear.

It is better to keep your mouth shut and appear stupid than to open it and remove all doubt.

Soap and education are not as sudden as a massacre but they are more deadly in the long run.

Get your facts first, and then you can distort them as much as you please.

Don't part with your illusions. When they are gone, you may still exist, but you have ceased to live.

Be careful to get out of an experience all the wisdom that is in it—not like the cat that sits down on a hot stove. She will never sit down on a hot stove lid again—and that is well; but also she will never sit down on a cold one anymore.

There never was a good war or a bad peace.
BENJAMIN FRANKLIN

The first hundred years are the hardest.
AMERICAN SOLDIERS in France, 1917–20

The ability to get to the verge of war without getting into war is the necessary art. If you cannot master it, you inevitably get into wars. If you try to run away from it, if you are scared to go to the brink, you are lost.   JOHN FOSTER DULLES

Mankind must put an end to war or war will put an end to mankind.   JOHN F. KENNEDY

War is too important to trust to generals.
GEORGES CLEMENCEAU

No plan survives contact with the enemy.
FIELD MARSHAL HELMUTH CARL
BERNARD VON MOLTKE

When eating an elephant take one bite at a time.
GENERAL CREIGHTON W. ABRAMS

> Though fraud in other activities be detestable, in
> the management of war it is laudable and glori-
> ous, and he who overcomes an enemy by fraud is
> as much to be praised as he who does so by force.
> NICCOLO MACHIAVELLI

Jaw-jaw is better than war-war.
HAROLD MACMILLAN

> You can no more win a war than you can win an
> earthquake.   JEANETTE RANKIN

The quickest way of ending a war is to lose it.
GEORGE ORWELL

A man bites off more trouble than he can chew when he doesn't do what his wife wants. You better believe it. SATCHEL PAIGE

You cannot pluck roses without fear of thorns, nor can you enjoy a fair wife without danger of horns. BENJAMIN FRANKLIN

Never tell. Not if you love your wife. . . . In fact, if your old lady walks in on you, deny it. Yeah. Just flat out and she'll believe it: "I'm tellin' ya. This chick came downstairs with a sign around her neck 'Lay on Top of Me Or I'll Die.' I didn't know what I was gonna do . . ." LENNY BRUCE

When a man steals your wife, there is no better revenge than to let him keep her. SACHA GUITRY

A husband should not insult his wife publicly, at parties. He should insult her in the privacy of the home. JAMES THURBER

Never feel remorse for what you have thought about your wife. She has thought much worse things about you.   JEAN ROSTAND

Never be unfaithful to a lover, except with your wife.   P. J. O'ROURKE

Money and women. They're two of the strongest things in the world. The things you do for a woman you wouldn't do for anything else. Same with money. SATCHEL PAIGE

One should never trust a woman who tells one her real age. A woman who would tell that would tell anything. OSCAR WILDE

Do not let any sweet-talking woman beguile your good sense with the fascinations of her shape. It's your barn she's after. HESIOD

There are only three things to be done with a woman. You can love her, suffer for her, or turn her into literature. LAWRENCE DURRELL

There's no such thing, you know, as picking out the best woman: it's only a question of comparative badness, brother. PLAUTUS

If you are rude to your ex-husband's new wife at your daughter's wedding, you will make her feel

smug. Comfortable. If you are charming and po-
lite, you will make her feel uncomfortable. Which
do you want to do?

MISS MANNERS (JUDITH MARTIN)

The only way to behave to a woman is to make
love to her if she is pretty, and to someone else if
she is plain. OSCAR WILDE

Choose not a woman or linen cloth by the candle.
JAMES SANFORD

Tell a female she's thin and she's yours for life.
ANNE BERNAYS

Never tell a woman she doesn't look good in some
article of clothing she has just purchased.

LEWIS GRIZZARD

o-o-o-o-o-o-o-o-o-o-o-o-o-o-o-o-o-o-o-o-o-o-o-o-o-o-o-o-o-o-o-o-o-o

Women, then, are only children of a larger growth; they
have an entertaining tattle, and sometimes wit; but for
solid reasoning, good sense, I never knew in my life one
that had it, or who reasoned or acted consequentially too

four and twenty hours together. Some little passion or humour always breaks in upon their best resolutions. Their beauty neglected or controverted, their age increased or their supposed understandings depreciated, instantly kindles their little passions, and overturns any system of consequential conduct, that in their most reasonable moments they might have been capable of forming. A man of sense only trifles with them, plays with them, humours and flatters them, as he does with a sprightly forward child; but he neither consults them about, nor trusts them with serious matters; though he often makes them believe that he does both; which is the thing in the world that they are proud of; for they love mightily to be dabbling in business (which, by the way, they always spoil); and being justly distrustful, that men in general look upon them in a trifling light, they almost adore that man who talks more seriously to them, and who seems to consult and trust them; I say, who seems; for weak men really do, but wise men only seem to do it. No flattery is either too high or too low for them. They will greedily swallow the highest, and gratefully accept the lowest; and you may safely flatter any woman from her understanding down to the exquisite taste of her fan.

LORD CHESTERFIELD to his son

Never be possessive. If a female friend lets on that she is going out with another man, be kind and understanding. If she says she would like to go out with the Dallas Cowboys, including the coaching staff, the same rule applies. Tell her: "Kath, you just go right ahead and do what you feel is right." Unless you actually care for her, in which case you must see to it that she has no male contact whatsoever.   BRUCE JAY FRIEDMAN

He gets on best with women who has learned to get on without them.   AMBROSE BIERCE

Don't tell a woman she's pretty; tell her there's no other woman like her, and all roads will open to you.   JULES RENARD

Stay away from girls who cry a lot or who look like they get pregnant easily or have careers.
   P. J. O'ROURKE

Never date a woman whose father calls her "Princess." Chances are she believes it.   WES SMITH

There is nothing so awkward as courting a woman whilst she is making sausages.

LAURENCE STERNE

Hit at the girl whenever possible.

BILL TILDEN (on how to play mixed doubles)

A woman's best protection is a little money of her own. CLARE BOOTH LUCE

Keep a diary and one day it'll keep you.

MAE WEST

No woman should ever be quite accurate about her age. It looks so calculating. OSCAR WILDE

My advice to the women's clubs of America is to raise more hell and fewer dahlias.

JAMES MCNEILL WHISTLER

The most important thing a woman can have— next to talent, of course—is her hairdresser.

JOAN CRAWFORD

Boys don't make passes at female smartasses.
LETTY COTTIN POGREBIN

Be touchable and kissable.   MARABEL MORGAN

Virtue is its own reward.   PHYLLIS SCHLAFLY

o-o-o-o-o-o-o-o-o-o-o-o-o-o-o-o-o-o-o-o-o-o-o-o-o-o-o-o-o-o-o-o-o-o-o

Literature cannot be the business of a woman's life, and it ought not to be. The more she is engaged in her proper duties, the less leisure she will have for it, even as an accomplishment and recreation. To those duties you have not yet been called, and when you are you will be less eager for celebrity.
ROBERT SOUTHEY to Charlotte Brönté

o-o-o-o-o-o-o-o-o-n-o-o-o o o-o-o-u-o-o-o-o-o-o-o-o-o-o-o-o-o-o-o-o-o

My advice to girls: first, don't smoke—to excess; second, don't drink—to excess; third, don't marry —to excess.   MARK TWAIN

Loving an old bachelor is always a no-win situation.   JEAN HARRIS

A girl whose cheeks are covered with paint
Has an advantage with me over one whose ain't.

OGDEN NASH

Beware of men on airplanes. The minute a man reaches thirty thousand feet, he immediately becomes consumed by distasteful sexual fantasies which involve doing uncomfortable things in those tiny toilets. These men should not be encouraged, their fantasies are sadly low-rent and unimaginative. Affect an aloof, cool demeanor as soon as any man tries to draw you out. Unless, of course, he's the pilot. CYNTHIA HEIMEL

From birth to age eighteen a girl needs good parents; from eighteen to thirty-five she needs good looks; from thirty-five to fifty-five she needs a good personality; from fifty-five on, she needs good cash. SOPHIE TUCKER

A woman, if she has the misfortune of knowing anything, should conceal it as well as she can. JANE AUSTEN

The more you act like a lady, the more he'll act like a gentleman. SYDNEY BIDDLE BARROWS

Want him to be more of a man? Try being more of a woman! COTY PERFUME AD

Ladies, here's a hint: if you're playing against a friend who has big boobs, bring her to the net and make her hit backhand volleys. That's the hardest shot for the well-endowed.

BILLIE JEAN KING

Don't die. WILLIAM M. GAINES

◇-◇

1. Avoid fried foods, which angry up the blood.

2. If your stomach disputes you, lie down and pacify it with cool thoughts.

3. Keep the juices flowing by jangling around gently as you move.

4. Go very light on the vices, such as carrying on in society. The social ramble ain't restful.

5. Avoid running at all times.

6. Don't look back. Something might be gaining on you.

SATCHEL PAIGE

◠-◠

Rule Number 1 is, don't sweat the small stuff. Rule Number 2 is, it's all small stuff. And if you can't fight and you can't flee, flow.

DR. ROBERT S. ELIOT

Be nice to people on the way up, because you'll meet them on the way down. WILSON MIZNER

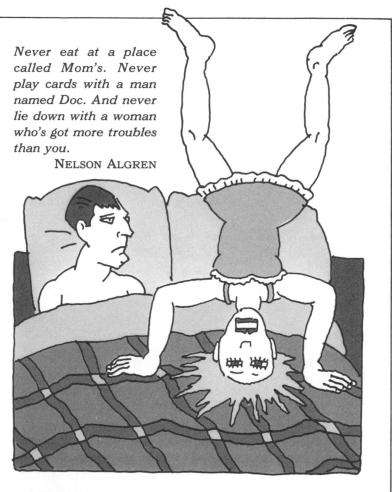

Never eat at a place called Mom's. Never play cards with a man named Doc. And never lie down with a woman who's got more troubles than you.

NELSON ALGREN

In the fight between you and the world, back the world. FRANK ZAPPA

o-o-o-o-o-o-o-o-o-o-o-o-o-o-o-o-o-o-o-o-o-o-o-o-o-o-o-o-o-o-o-o-o-o-o

Look out for yourself, or they'll pee on your grave.
L. B. MAYER to Mervyn LeRoy

o o o o-o-o-o-o-o-o-o-o-o-o-o-o-o-o-o-o-o-o-o-o-o-o-o-o-o-o-o-o-o-o-o

The other line moves faster. This applies to all lines—bank, supermarket, tollbooth, customs, and so on. And don't try to change lines. The Other Line—the one you were in originally—will then move faster. BARBARA ETTORE

Don't play for safety—it's the most dangerous thing in the world. HUGH WALPOLE

Eat not to dullness. Drink not to elevation.
BENJAMIN FRANKLIN

To get it right, be born with luck or else make it. Never give up. A little money helps, but what really gets it right is to *never face the facts*.
RUTH GORDON

∘-∘

"When in Rome do as the Romans do" is probably based on the advice given to St. Augustine by St. Ambrose: "When I am at Rome I fast on Saturdays; when I am at Milan I do not. Follow the custom of the church where you happen to be."

∘-∘

You gotta keep changing. Shirts, old ladies, whatever.   NEIL YOUNG

> Don't take yourself too seriously. And don't be too serious about not taking yourself too seriously.   HOWARD OGDEN

Don't worry. Be happy.   BOBBY MCFERRIN

> The first principle is that you must not fool yourself—and you are the easiest person to fool.
> RICHARD FEYNMAN

What you do not want done to yourself, do not do to others.   CONFUCIUS

○-○

Nothing is good in moderation. You cannot know good in anything until you have torn the heart out of it by excess.
OSCAR WILDE to André Gide

○-○

Do not do unto others as you would that they should do unto you. Their tastes may not be the same.
GEORGE BERNARD SHAW

Do unto yourself as your neighbors do unto themselves and look pleasant.
GEORGE ADE

What is worth doing is worth the trouble of asking somebody to do it.
AMBROSE BIERCE

Be kind and considerate to others, depending somewhat upon who they are.
DON HEROLD

You ought to take the bull between the teeth.
SAMUEL GOLDWYN

Things are seldom what they seem.
Skim milk masquerades as cream.
W. S. GILBERT

Don't call someone a bad name if they have a loaded pistol; don't call your girlfriend Tina if her name is Vivien.   GEORGE UNDERWOOD

It's not whether you win or lose, it's how you play the game.   GRANTLAND RICE

Grantland Rice can go to hell as far as I'm concerned.   GENE AUTRY

It is not whether you win or lose, but who gets the blame.   BLAINE NYE

"How you play the game" is for college boys. When you're playing for money, winning is the only thing that counts.   LEO DUROCHER

Be somebody. Know that a bunch of guys will do anything you tell 'em. Have your own way or nothin'.
          EDWARD G. ROBINSON in *Little Caesar*
          (screenplay by Francis Edwards Faragoh)

Better bend than break.   H. G. BOHN

It is better to be beautiful than to be good, but it is better to be good than to be ugly.

OSCAR WILDE

o-o-o-o-o-o-o-o-o-o-o-o-o-o-o-o-o-o-o-o-o-o-o-o-o-o-o-o-o-o-o-o-o-o

HOW TO BEHAVE IN AN ELEVATOR

1. Face forward.
2. Fold hands in front.
3. Do not make eye contact.
4. Watch the numbers.
5. Don't talk to anyone you don't know.
6. Stop talking with anyone you do know when anyone you don't know enters the elevator.
7. Avoid brushing bodies.

LAYNE LONGFELLOW

o-o-o-o-o-o-o-o-o-o-o-o-o o-o-o-o-o-o-o-o-o-o-o-o-o-o-o-o-o-o-o-o-o-o-o

You're only here for a short visit. Don't hurry, don't worry. And be sure to smell the flowers along the way.

WALTER HAGEN

If you're going to do something wrong, at least enjoy it.

LEO ROSTEN

Don't ask the barber whether you need a haircut.
DANIEL S. GREENBERG

Have a blast while you last. HOLLIS STACY

There are two great rules of life: never tell everything at once. KEN VENTURI

You've got to be very careful if you don't know where you are going, because you might not get there. YOGI BERRA

Don't let the same dog bite you twice.
CHUCK BERRY

Be civil to all; sociable to many; familiar with few. BENJAMIN FRANKLIN

Sleep not when others speak, sit not when others stand, speak not when you should hold your peace, walk not on when others stop.
GEORGE WASHINGTON

My motto is, "Contented with little, yet wishing for more." CHARLES LAMB

It is better to be rich and healthy than poor and sick.   DAVE BARRY

Beware of Greeks bearing gifts, colored men looking for loans, and whites who understand the Negro.   ADAM CLAYTON POWELL, JR.

It is a sin to believe evil of others, but it is seldom a mistake.   H. L. MENCKEN

Dare to be naive.   R. BUCKMINSTER FULLER

Don't ever prophesy; for if you prophesy wrong, nobody will forget it and if you prophesy right, nobody will remember it.   JOSH BILLINGS

The first and great commandment is, Don't let them scare you.   ELMER DAVIS

Believe nothing, no matter where you read it, or who said it—even if I have said it—unless it agrees with your own reason and your own common sense.   THE BUDDHA

Everything should be made as simple as possible, but not simpler.   ALBERT EINSTEIN

When you arrive at a fork in the road, take it.
                                                    YOGI BERRA

It is an immense advantage to have done nothing, but one should not abuse it. COMTE DE RIVAROL

Don't compromise yourself. You are all you've got.   JANIS JOPLIN

What, me worry?   ALFRED E. NEUMAN

It is fatal to look hungry. It makes people want to kick you.   GEORGE ORWELL

Leave undone whatever you hesitate to do.
                                                YOSHIDA KANKO

Resist much, obey little.   WALT WHITMAN

Honesty is the best policy and spinach is the best vegetable.   "POPEYE"

When the going gets weird, the weird turn pro.
                              HUNTER S. THOMPSON

Don't let your mouth write a check that your tail can't cash.   BO DIDDLEY

Take what you can use and let the rest go by.
                              KEN KESEY

Nothing risqué, nothing gained.
                              ALEXANDER WOOLLCOTT

If you cannot catch a bird of paradise, better take a wet hen   NIKITA KHRUSHCHEV

When the tides of life turn against you,
And the current upsets your boat,
Don't waste those tears on what might have been;
Just lay on your back and float.
                              ART CARNEY as Ed Norton
                              in *The Honeymooners*

If it ain't broke, don't fix it.   OLD ADAGE

If it might break, don't go near it.

HERBERT STEIN

The first thing to do when you're being stalked by an angry mob with raspberries is to release a tiger.

JOHN CLEESE

Try to be one of the people on whom nothing is lost.

HENRY JAMES

Why be influenced by a person when you already are one?

MARTIN MULL

"No harm can come to a good man in life or death."— Socrates

HUGH DOWNS

The best ＿＿ is no ＿＿ at all.

JOHN CAGE

Syzygy, inexorable, pancreatic, phantasmagoria—anyone who can use those four words in one sentence will never have to do manual labor.

W. P. KINSELLA

Things could be a lot worse.

JOYCE CAROL OATES

Forget goals. Value the process.   JIM BOUTON

I live by Louis Pasteur's advice that "Chance favors the prepared mind," and my own, "The two most common elements in the known universe are hydrogen and stupidity."

HARLAN ELLISON

"Do-so" is more important than "say-so."

PETE SEEGER

An ounce of sequins can be worth a pound of home cooking.   MARILYN VOS SAVANT

Revenge, duplicity, and betrayal.

ROY LICHTENSTEIN

Think for yourself and question authority.

TIMOTHY LEARY

Be a moving target.   RAOUL LIONEL FELDER

"Raise a standard to which the wise and honest can repair; the event is in the hand of God"— George Washington   PHYLLIS SCHLAFLY

You can never be too paranoid.

C. E. CRIMMINS

If you think you can, you can. And if you think you can't, you're right.   MARY KAY ASH

Two would actually do it—two magic words that could replace all the religions in the world—two wonderful words that embrace all the powers and all of the energy we need to survive with each other and with our planet and with all the world's living creatures—*don't hurt*.   ROGER CARAS

When you get there, there is no there there. But there *will be* a pool.   DAVID ZUCKER

Pressed for rules and verities,
All I recollect are these:
Feed a cold and starve a fever.
Argue with no true believer.
Think too-long is never-act.
Scratch a myth and find a fact.

PHYLLIS MCGINLEY

Never work before breakfast; if you have to work before breakfast, eat your breakfast first.

JOSH BILLINGS

One of the best ways of avoiding necessary and even urgent tasks is to seem to be busily employed on things that are already done.

JOHN KENNETH GALBRAITH

Housework, if it is done right, can kill you.

JOHN SKOW

What the hell do you want to work for somebody else for? Work for yourself!

IRVING BERLIN's advice to young songwriter George Gershwin

It is better to have loafed and lost than never to have loafed at all.   JAMES THURBER

If you don't have enough time to accomplish something, consider the work finished once it's begun.

JOHN CAGE

The one important thing I have learned over the years is the difference between taking one's work seriously and taking one's self seriously. The first is imperative and the second is disastrous.

MARGOT FONTEYN

What you want to do is not go to work. You're not missing a thing. The worst thing I did was start work young.

JIMMY BRESLIN

My advice to any young writer is: become an editor. You'll do less work, have less pressure, have more influence, make more money, and best of all: you get to tell others what to do instead of having to do all that rotten research and writing yourself.   BOB CHIEGER

A good many young writers make the mistake of enclosing a stamped, self-addressed envelope big enough for the manuscript to come back in. This is too much of a temptation to the editor.
                                         RING LARDNER

Find another profession to be young in.
                                         JOE QUEENAN

The only advice I have to give a young novelist is to fuck a really good agent.   JOHN CHEEVER

Always remember that if editors were so damned smart, they would know how to dress.
                                         DAVE BARRY

○-○

Let wife and child perish, and lay bricks for your last
crust, rather than part with an iota of your [copy]rights.
GEORGE BERNARD SHAW to Sean O'Casey

○-○

A little inaccuracy sometimes saves tons of expla-
nation. SAKI

When a thought is too weak to be expresssed
simply, simply drop it. VAUVENARGUES

○-○

A young Ben Hecht received the following advice from a
newspaper editor: "When you write never get too fancy.
Never put one foot on the mantelpiece, and be sure your
style is so honest that you can put the word *shit* in any
sentence without fear of consequence."

○-○

If you would be pungent, be brief; for it is with
words as with sunbeams. The more they are con-
densed, the deeper they burn.
ROBERT SOUTHEY

Responding to criticism is a foolish thing for a writer to do, and an unpleasant one. It is much better to read only the advertisements of your work and to note, briefly, your royalty reports. These will tell you how popular you are. How good you are, or are not, is a thing you should know only too well yourself.   BEN HECHT

Read what you've written aloud—you'll learn the rhythms that work for you.   NAT HENTOFF

Though I'd been taught at our dining room table about the solar system and knew the earth revolved around the sun, and our moon around us, I never found out the moon didn't come up in the west until I was a writer and Herschel Brickell, the literary critic, told me after I misplaced it in a story. He said valuable words to me about my new profession: "Always be sure you get your moon in the right part of the sky."
      EUDORA WELTY

I was taking a course with Lionel Trilling and wrote a paper for him with an opening sentence that contained a parenthesis. He returned the paper with a wounding reprimand: "Never, never begin an essay with a parenthesis in the first sentence." Ever since then, I've made a point of starting out with a parenthesis in the first sentence.   CYNTHIA OZICK

○-○

Try medicine, why don't you! Lots to keep you busy, and lots to make you think. The great thing is—you get to forget yourself a lot of the time.
                    WILLIAM CARLOS WILLIAMS to Robert Coles

○-○

One begins with two people on a stage, and one of them had better say something pretty damn quick.
                                                    MOSS HART

Go on writing plays, my boy. One of these days one of these London producers will go into his office and say to his secretary, "Is there a play from Shaw this morning?" and when she says, "No," he will say, "Well, then we'll have to start

on the rubbish." And that's your chance, my boy.
                                                    GEORGE BERNARD SHAW
                                                    to a young playwright

Don't write stage directions. If it is not apparent what the character is trying to accomplish by saying the line, telling us *how* the character said it, or whether or not she moved to the couch, isn't going to aid the case.   DAVID MAMET

Never fear [the public] or despise it. Coax it, charm it, interest it, stimulate it, shock it now and then if you must, make it laugh, make it cry, but above all . . . never, never, never bore the hell out of it.   NOEL COWARD

Opening night . . . you will find a sizable number of people with severe respiratory infections who have, it appears, defied their doctors, torn aside oxygen tents, evaded the floor nurses at various hospitals, and courageously made their way to the theater to enjoy the play—the Discreet Choker and the Straight Cougher.   MIKE NICHOLS

If the critics unanimously take exception to one particular scene it is advisable to move that scene to a more conspicuous place in the program.

NOEL COWARD

<hr>

A young Harvard graduate on his way to Oxford on a fellowship called on T. S. Eliot in his office at Faber & Faber. After a cordial but somewhat formal interview, Eliot rose to bid his young guest goodbye: "Let me see, forty years ago I went from Harvard to Oxford. What advice can I give you?" As the young man waited anxiously, Eliot paused as if in search of the perfect bit of wisdom, then said, "Have you any long underwear?"

<hr>

In a novel the hero can lay ten girls and marry a virgin for the finish. In a movie that is not allowed. The villain can lay anybody he wants, have as much fun as he wants cheating and stealing, getting rich, and whipping the servants. But you have to shoot him in the end. When he falls with a bullet in the forehead it is advisable that he clutch at the Gobelin tapestry on the wall and bring it down over his head like a symbolic shroud.

Also, covered by such a tapestry, the actor does not have to hold his breath while being photographed as a dead man.   HERMAN MANKIEWICZ

The Movie Hero's Ten Commandments:
1. A man stands alone.
2. A man stands by his friends.
3. A man protects his family.
4. A man loves doing his work well.
5. A man is at home out of doors.
6. A man shares and plays fair.
7. A man speaks his mind.
8. A man hoards his smiles.
9. A man follows his dreams.
10. What he's got is what he is.

RICHARD CORLISS

o-o-o-o-o-o-o-o-o-o-o-o-o-o-o-o-o-o-o-o-o-o-o-o-o-o-o-o-o-o-o-o-o-o-o-o

In the afternoons, Gertrude Stein and I used to go antique hunting in the local shops, and I remember once asking her if she thought I should become a writer. In the typically cryptic way we were all so enchanted with, she said, "No." I took that to mean yes and sailed for Italy the next day.   WOODY ALLEN

o-o-o-o-o-o-o-o-o-o-o-o-o-o-o-o-o-o-o-o-o-o-o-o-o-o-o-o-o-o-o-o-o-o-o-o

INDEX

Marquis, Don, 65, 67, 68, 122, 152
Marr, Dave, 118
Marshall, Gen. George C., 50
Martial, Marcus Valerius, 166
Martin, Billy, 46, 171
Martin, Dean, 78, 116
Martin, Judith (Miss Manners), 251
Martin, Steve, 104
Mary, Queen of England, 171
Marx, Chico, 101
Marx, Groucho, 152, 155
Marx, Harpo, 144, 156
Masson, Tom, 16
Masters, Dr. William H., 70
Mathewson, Christy, 47
Matisse, Henri, 42
Matthews, Christopher, 91, 191
Maude, John, 38
Maugham, W. Somerset, 94, 95, 145, 146
Maurois, André, 30
Maverick, "Pappy," 87, 92
Mayer, Edith, 88
Mayer, Louis B., 21, 63, 88, 261
Mayo, Dr. William, 124

Mazursky, Paul, 73
Mead, Margaret, 206
Medawar, Peter, 220
Meisner, Sanford, 21
Melchior, Lauritz, 174
Menaker, Daniel, 67
Mencken, H. L., 77, 103, 152, 184, 267
Merrill, Robert, 174
Michals, Duane, 57
Miles, Sylvia, 29
Milhaud, Darius, 53
Miller, Arjay, 62
Miller, Arthur, 91
Miller, Bryan, 93
Miller, Henry, 101, 112
Milligan, Spike, 169, 223
Milne, A. A., 152
Milstein, Nathan, 147
Minkow, Barry, 65
"Miss Piggy," 94, 99, 168, 238
"Mr. Ed," 182
Mitford, Jessica, 239
Mizner, Wilson, 35, 259
Moltke, Helmuth Carl Bernard von, 246
Mondale, Walter, 203
Monet, Claude, 41
Monk, Thelonious, 173, 175

ABOUT THE AUTHOR

Jon Winokur, the author of several books, including *Writers on Writing* and *Zen to Go,* lives and works in Pacific Palisades, California. He advises you to read this book.